Italian Stories

Udara
(Nino Caputo)

Italian Stories

Published by *Triratna InHouse Publications*
www.*triratna-inhouse-publications.org*

Cover image Grassano in Basilicata, Southern Italy, 2004 © Udara

TRIRATNA
INHOUSE
PUBLICATIONS

Contents

When I started writing twenty years ago, I was given the advice "write about what you know".

So that's what I've tried to do.

- Udara

The Piano

I heard my sister shouting and went at once to my window. She had one of the village boys by the scruff of his neck and was marching him towards the house.

'Thief, thief,' she screamed. 'Disgraceful thief!'

What a pitiful sight. He must have been eight years old, nine at the most. My room is on the third floor and even at that distance there was no mistaking his ragged clothes, patched and darned repeatedly to hold them together. I could have stepped out onto the balcony for a better look but I didn't want them to see me so I stood behind the shutters instead, watching. Katrina towered over him; she was wearing one of her long white summer dresses; her hair had become unpinned in her fury and hung down, partly obscuring her face.

'Thief, thief,' she shouted it again. Then slapped the back of his head with her free hand.

Katrina's haughtiness was continuing to cause great embarrassment for my father, although neither Allessandro, nor myself, being her brothers, could escape being compromised by her actions. It began soon after mother died. My sister found her asleep in her chair. It was a year ago almost to the day and a week before Katrina's fourteenth birthday. She went to wake her then ran out into the garden screaming. I was gathering figs with Father, from the tree against the south wall. Her face was white and she was crying out. "Please come, please come. I can't wake mother."

The autopsy showed a tumour the size of an orange in mother's brain. No one had suspected anything even though she was becoming more and more irritable and short-tempered. Father said it was something women went through when they reached a certain age and that it would pass. He is not the same man without her.

The top of his moon head appeared from beneath the portico. He walked down the stone steps and waited. His shoulders were hunched from sitting over his desk. It was late summer, coming onto autumn, and he had been working on his accounts, calculating how we will live this coming year from the rents the peasants pay us for their scraps of land and the hovels they live in. He took off his spectacles and rubbed his eyes with the back of his hands; then put them back on, as though somehow it would enable him to comprehend the scene more clearly. My sister let go of the little boy and stood before him, clenching and unclenching her fists.

'Look, Father, look,' she shouted. Pointing to the boy's bulging pockets.

The boy looked up at my father, then back down at the ground, shame-faced. My father shook his head, more in disbelief than because he was trying to humiliate him.

'I found him in our woods,' shouted my sister. 'He was stealing our chestnuts.'

My stomach turned. I stepped back from the window and closed the shutters to keep out the sound of her insane accusations but her voice continued to find its way into my room, slightly muffled. A book of music manuscripts lay on my desk; I sat down and began flicking through the pages to distract myself. Then, unable to concentrate, I grabbed my jacket from the back of my chair and went to leave the house.

I found Allessandro, my older brother, standing on the landing; it was obvious from the look on his face that he had also witnessed the same sorry sight.

'If this was Russia,' he said. 'The peasants would be looking to lynch her.'

My brother has a knowledge of the world and a confidence that I don't have; he was on holiday too; for the past three years he has lived in Turin where he is studying law. I am very cautious of my brother; so is my father. He and Allessandro have hardly spoken since mother died, before that they quarrelled endlessly. Allessandro has become a communist; it all began when he moved to Turin. He hardly spends any of the allowance Father sends him and instead shares a room with another student in a poor part of the city. Allessandro says our government is a disgrace, that the war with Abyssinia is a massacre, that simple innocent people are being murdered with poison gas. Father says that it's nonsense; that the war gives our people hope and what would they have without it? He fears that Allessandro will be arrested, perhaps sent to an even more remote part of Italy than this. But what he fears most is that our family will be compromised. Allessandro says that the men are going to fight because it is the only way they can feed their families. He keeps quiet now, not because his views have changed but out of respect for our grief.

I said, 'I'm going for a walk.'

I intended to go to the vineyard. I knew it would be another month before the grapes ripened and that it would be deserted. My brother gave me one of his looks, it was obvious that I would be leaving by the back door; he knew it and my embarrassment continued to grow. I ran down the flights of marble stairs hardly touching the iron banister with my hand. Then, just as I turned to leave the hallway, the front door slammed behind me. I looked round and saw my father and sister standing either side of the little boy.

My father said, 'Ah, this is my son, Donato.'

I couldn't believe Father had brought him inside. It was a mistake on his part; he just didn't know how to act with the peasants. I realised that he was trying to make light of the whole incident, while trying to appease my sister at the same time. The boy looked up at me for a moment; his eyes were big and round, his hair short, cropped close to his head and just beginning to grow into tight curls. I pretended not to know anything about the chestnuts and acted as though he was a guest of my father's. I held out my hand. He shook it lightly hardly raising his eyes from the floor, then tugged at the sleeves of his shirt which hung down over his hands. The shirt swamped him; he seemed lost inside it. The tails were pulled out from his trousers, no doubt by my sister's rough handling and his trousers too were rolled up and rested on his boots. I wondered what he must have thought of me, standing there in my white shirt and cotton trousers, my jacket casually slung over my arm. I tried not to stare at his patches, tried not to compare myself with him. He began to look at me uncomprehendingly, his eyes frightened and bulging, like the birds that sometimes fly indoors unintentionally through an open window, then beat themselves against the walls in their confusion trying to escape.

Father said, 'What is your name, boy?'

The way he said "boy" shamed me. I looked at Father; his expression showed regret immediately, unlike my sister who seemed to grow larger in authority.

'Pietrino,' he replied. His Adam's apple rose and fell in a swallow.

'Pietrino,' my sister repeated, glaring at him.

Little Pietro, I realised by the way he said it, the affection his family surely felt for him and wished I could stop her ridiculing him. He began looking around, first at the marble floor, blinking, then at the stairs winding themselves up through the centre of the house, at the doors leading off the hall and the walnut table with the mirror hanging above. I had sometimes walked through his part of the village in the evenings, past the hovels where clouds of wood-smoke clung over the squat chimneys and seen boys and girls Pietrino's age sitting outside the open doorways; I had glanced inside surreptitiously at the crude brick floors, seen a corner of the matrimonial bed and caught the odour of food-cooking mixed with the smell of the goats and donkeys tethered to the walls outside, waiting to be brought in for the night.

My father said, 'Donato is on holiday from school.'

I shrugged and looked at him in disbelief. The more Father tried to put Pietrino at ease the more awkward he became. 'Yes,' he continued despite my embarrassment. 'He finishes in two years, then he will study music.'

Pietrino began staring at my hands. I folded my fingers over each other. No matter how hard I tried, I couldn't help comparing myself with him. His hands and fingers were squat, his nails black and broken. He could have wielded an axe I'm sure, and probably did. He was strong enough to have struggled free from my sister and run off, but he wouldn't have. His people have a fear of our kind, as though our position is god-given. I thought of the children I saw everyday with their hoes and mattocks slung over their shoulders, following their parents and pack mules back and forth from the country. A silence fell over the four of us.

Father noticed, he put his hand on Pietrino's shoulder to dispel the awkwardness and said, 'Come.' He walked with him towards the music room and gestured for us to follow. Father's sense of etiquette was always misguided. I knew that he wanted him to leave the house as though nothing had happened. A difficult task; the impression my sister had made would be impossible to eradicate. I could see why he chose the music room. Where else could we have gone? The kitchen might have been better but Madelena, our housekeeper, would have been there working. It would not have done for her to have seen us in this situation and besides, talk of the incident would have spread all over the village by evening. No, the music room was better; it was private, unlike the hall where she could have entered at any moment and much less grand than the other rooms.

The piano was just as I had left it, with the lid open and the keys facing us. The French windows were open too; the curtains hung still and lifeless either side. A shaft of light poured in and lit a square on the marble floor. This room had not always been the music room; the piano used to be on the third floor, to the rear of the bedrooms. It was mother's idea to bring it down here. I remember years ago, when I was still quite young, she was standing by the door and the sun was pouring in through the French windows, just as it was that day. She pointed to the windows, then at the square of light the sun made on the floor and said, "That's where I want it, that's where I want my piano". Father called in workmen the following day; he never denied her anything. They removed the legs and placed the body into a great padded glove. Other workmen removed the window to make room and lowered the piano down with ropes and blocks and tackle. Then they brought it back inside and reassembled it exactly where mother wanted. When she played, it was as though her music poured out through the windows into the world outside. It was here that she first taught me to play and here that my sister found her dead in her chair.

Katrina hardly ever came into this room now. She folded her hands tightly around her chest and pressed her lips together. Her fury seemed to have abated slightly and a look of confusion took over her face. I'm sure she'd expected Father to settle the matter outside with a few harsh words, to have made Pietrino empty his pockets in front of her, then sent him off. That way she could have strutted off to her room vindicated.

Father said, 'Pietrino, sit down,' and gestured towards mother's chair. My sister's eyes filled with tears immediately. He realised his mistake and looked at me. I was shocked, but I knew it was forgetfulness, an oversight on his part. Fortunately, there were footsteps outside in the hall, then a knock and Allessandro walked in; he looked about him taking the scene in at a glance, then acknowledged us. Pietrino sat perched on the edge of mother's chair as though afraid his rags would soil the pale upholstery. Allessandro smiled at him. Pietrino looked up, cautiously at first, then gazed at him as though he were an older brother. My sister turned her back angrily, then stormed towards the French windows and stood there staring out. My brother is someone who knows his own mind; he does his thinking for himself. That is what sets him apart from us. At that moment I realised Pietrino had found himself an ally in this trap he had been dragged into and I felt glad.

Father said, 'Katrina found Pietrino in the woods; he wandered there by mistake.'

He looked towards me as though for support hardly acknowledging Allessandro. I shrugged my shoulders and shook my head as if to say, "Well yes, perhaps I believe that's what happened."

Then he stooped onto one knee in front of Pietrino, so that their faces were level. 'You know where the road sweeps in front of the woods?' he said.

Pietrino nodded.

'Well,' continued my father. 'The land beyond the road is the property of the house.' It was obvious he had not reckoned on Allessandro being in the room and began to stumble over his words, the way he does when he is nervous. I could see he was trying to play the kind, liberal landowner. That he intended to persuade Pietrino to acknowledge his error, then gently admonish him and send him on his way in the hope it would appease my sister. Allessandro could see this too; we looked at each other embarrassed.

'It's easy for anyone to make a mistake,' Father said. 'I can understand that; it's not a big thing.'

Katrina continued to stand silently at the window with her back turned looking up at the sky. Pietrino looked about him, tears formed in his eyes, then he turned to my brother. I wished that he could have looked at me in the same way, that somehow, I could have given him the same reassurance.

'How do you think the chestnut trees first came to be?' Father asked.

I wondered what kind of moralistic tale he was trying to spin; I thought that he was going to bring God into this or talk about our grandfathers. I felt sickened.

Father smiled, his face just inches from Pietrino's, 'Well, can you tell me?'

I wanted to shout at Father, say, 'Who do you think you are to put him through this ordeal?'

Pietrino blinked his eyes hesitatingly and looked up at Allessandro, then he opened his mouth and began to speak, 'First a chestnut falls from a tree.' His dialect was drawled and archaic, barely recognizable as Italian. 'Some chestnuts are eaten by animals, others are gathered by people and some rot but sometimes a chestnut is carried off and falls onto the earth where it sprouts shoots. If it is not rooted up by a wild boar or eaten by sheep or goats it grows into a tree.'

His innocence caused a silence to come over us. My father turned away and stared at the floor, too moved to speak.

Pietrino looked around the room awkwardly, not knowing what to do, then stood up. I thought he was going to leave but he just stood still, gaping at mother's piano as if he'd never seen a piano before. Then he stepped towards it as though inveigled by some spell and pressed one of the keys. A deep bass note broke the silence.

Katrina turned at once from the French windows and came storming towards us with both her fists clenched. 'Father, Father,' she screamed. 'How can you let him touch mother's piano?'

Father caught her wrist a moment before she struck Pietrino's face. She threw herself backwards, flapping like a dispatched chicken, beating Father with her free hand. Then she fell onto his chest crying… A storm had broken.

'I miss Mother,' she cried and continued to sob inconsolably.

Pietrino looked first at my sister, then at the rest of us, seeing us all just as we were, reduced to being ourselves in our grief. It was the one thing we had in common, his kind and ours.

Allessandro went to him; he placed a hand on his shoulder and led him out of the room. I knew he would walk back with him to the wood, that they would pick chestnuts together. I wished that it could have been me that went there with him, that I could be as sure of myself as Allessandro. Eventually Katrina calmed, she went to mother's chair and stood behind it. Then she rested her hands on its back.

Circle Dancing

It was late morning, heading towards noon. Andrea wondered whether to kiss his wife goodbye. She looked down at the baby and rocked her gently. It was agreed between them that she would get up for the babies while he slept. Andrea decided this, mostly because he was the provider. He picked his other daughter up from the floor and kissed her a couple of times on the cheek, then put her back down among her toys. Lydia looked up at him. He smiled at her. She didn't smile back, just looked down at the baby and carried on rocking her gently.

Andrea closed the door quietly and went downstairs to his bar. He took a cloth and carefully wiped down the shiny, stainless steel coffee machine, then pushed one of the levers. Steam hissed out. He looked at his watch. It was still a little early to open. He went to the lavatory, unzipped and urinated, then began pulling at himself. After a while he unfastened his belt, pulled some sheets of paper from the roll and sat down on the seat. He squeezed and kneaded his penis, in between long breaths until he ejaculated into the handful of paper. Some time passed, during which he reflected on his situation, then he wiped himself with the paper, pulled his trousers back up and washed his hands scrupulously.

The coffee machine reflected back his distorted image. Andrea never imagined marrying Lydia would end up like this. It showed in his face and he looked away quickly.

He unlocked the door, took the pole that stood to one side and went outside. The old man was standing across the street as usual, waiting for him to open. He had a copy of La Corriera folded under his arm and he was wearing the same suit he always wore. It had been a good suit once, beige, but now it hung badly over his out-of-shape body. Andrea pulled down the awning and shade immediately covered his tables. He went back inside, then reappeared with a cloth and a pile of ash-trays. He wiped each table and set down an ash-tray in the centre of each one. The old man sat down behind him.

'What will it be today?' Andrea asked, even though he already knew the answer. It was always a bottle of wine and a glass.

The old man said, 'Half a bottle of wine and a glass.' Then he drew his finger horizontally through the air, to indicate *half* a bottle. 'I have some business later, with my daughter.'

Andrea studied him carefully for a few seconds, then realized he was staring and turned away. He noticed the old man wasn't really so old, around fifty, less than fifty-five anyway and that his odour was unpleasant. A bath and a shave wouldn't do him any harm Andrea thought, then he started to wonder how a man could end up in a state like that. He went back inside, opened the bottle and placed it on a tray next to a glass and a saucer. He put a couple of Amoretti biscuits on the saucer and went back outside. The old man had opened his paper and gripped it tightly in front of his face, as though he was angry with it. Andrea set the tray down on the table, poured him a glass of wine and saw he was crying. It wasn't the first time this had happened, usually he ignored it but today he put his hand on the old man's shoulder.

He said, 'Take it easy, old man.'

The old man pressed his palms into his eyes and nodded. Andrea went back inside and watched over his tables through the window. A group of old men gathered around one. He served them some espressos. More men gathered inside. The place filled with the smell of smoke and coffee and talk, as the till slowly filled with money. Andrea looked out over the roof-tops opposite, at the mountains all around, and at the villages perched on top of them like islands. It had been a smart move, coming back home and opening the bar. There was only one other bar in the village. Hardly anyone went there now. It was shabby. He remembered the old man and looked his way again. The old man raised his glass, his hand trembled and a few drops of wine spilt onto his clothes.

D'Nunzio showed up with a bunch of friends, four young men and a couple of girls about half his age. They drew up a couple of extra chairs and crowded around one of the tables out on the pavement. D'Nunzio came inside and sat on one of the tall stools that lined the bar.

'I've brought along some of my colleagues from the Municipal Office,' he said. He rubbed his thumb and forefinger together and smiled. 'They have to spend their money somewhere.'

Andrea smiled back. 'What will it be?' he asked.

'A cappuccino and twenty Nazionali, but no hurry, serve the others first.'

Andrea went outside and scribbled their orders onto a pad. The girls joked and flirted with him. He came back in, loaded his tray and carried it out. Froth ran down the sides of the coffee cups. He took a pile of paninos from the cold display and took those outside too.

'Cappuccino and twenty Marlborough,' he said, pushing them across the counter towards D'Nunzio.

D'Nunzio reached into his pocket.

'On the house.' Andrea always gave him things on the house when he brought people to the bar.

'Very kind,' D'Nunzio replied. Then he loosened his tie and unfastened the pack of cigarettes. He tapped one out of the corner and pulled it out of the pack with his mouth, as though he were in a movie. Casablanca had just shown in the village and all the young men were lighting their cigarettes like Humphrey Bogart, D'Nunzio too, even though he wasn't so young. Someone started a Fiat across the street. Its exhaust back-fired. A mule tethered close-by spooked and eeawed a couple of times, then settled down. D'Nunzio looked around and shook his head.

'The peasants shouldn't be allowed to bring their mules into the Piazza,' he said. 'Anyone would think we were still living in the Dark Ages.' He lit his cigarette and leaned back on the stool, blowing smoke into the air, then shook his head again.

Andrea nodded in agreement, even though he had no problem with the mules and looked over D'Nunzio's shoulder, through the window to the old man. He was half way through his bottle, the paper lay rolled up on the table beside it and he was staring into space.

'What is it with the old man?' Andrea asked. 'Is he a widower or something?'

D'Nunzio laughed. 'Widower nothing,' he said. He laughed again as though Andrea had made a joke. 'No. Rumour is he mortgaged the apartment he owns with his daughter, and now the bank wants its money.'

A couple of young men showed up and sat at one of the tables out on the pavement. Andrea went out to them and took their order, then glanced at the old man. It wasn't decent, he thought, talking about him behind his back, especially laughing at him the way D'Nunzio did. He took out the young men's orders then returned to his place behind the bar.

The place was full of smoke. D'Nunzio grinned and sipped his cappuccino, then leaned over the bar. 'Do you want to hear about old Fabrizzio?' he said.

Andrea nodded and leaned forward, so close he could smell D'Nunzio's tobacco breath, unable to contain his curiosity.

'Matrimonial problems,' he whispered, then exploded into laughter.

Andrea stepped back, startled by the sudden outburst.

D'Nunzio grinned again and beckoned for him to come closer. The voices either side grew louder. 'Listen,' he said, as though he was going to tell him a secret.

Andrea cupped his hand over his ear and leaned towards him again.

'His background is not so different to your own. When Fabrizzio was a young man, not much more than a boy, he emigrated. There were some relations in New York who sponsored him. The grandfathers had some obligation to one another. Do you understand?'

Andrea said, 'Sure. Most things around here are decided according to family obligations. No one is ever really free to do what they want.'

Someone called out for a coffee. Andrea took it over. He came back, pressed the button on his till and dropped the money in. 'So, he emigrated, but what happened for him to end up like that?'

D'Nunzio flicked ash into the ash-tray and let his cigarette rest there. The smoke rose up in whorls.

'Fabrizzio became apprenticed to a butcher,' he said. 'He learnt the trade, then he worked hard for a few years and saved some money. It's a common story.' D'Nunzio narrowed his eyes, as though recalling something important. 'Yes, there are many similarities between you. You emigrated too, then returned and set up a business, only you learnt the bar trade. But you both went to New York.'

'No,' Andrea interrupted. 'I went to Toronto.'

'New York, Toronto, what's the difference?' his voice rose. 'If it wasn't for the years, you would have been neighbours.'

Andrea decided to let the error pass. 'So, then what happened to Fabrizzio?'

D'Nunzio made a face. 'I heard he tired of the American women, too disobedient. Then a girl from the village started writing to him. She sent him her photograph. He wasn't the only one she sent her photograph to.' He made the same face again... 'Thirty years ago, it was impossible for a woman to find a husband in these parts. The war, emigration, do you understand? In short, he lost his head.' D'Nunzio drew meaningfully on his cigarette. He let a few moments lapse. 'Are you sure you want to hear the rest?'

Andrea nodded.

'Fabrizzio set up his own butchers' shop, with an apartment up above where they lived, not unlike yourself.' He looked up at the ceiling.

Andrea looked up too and thought of Lydia and the babies.

'To begin with things went well. There was only one other butchers' shop in the village, but it was shabby. Fabrizzio had learned some style and brought it back with him. It showed in the way he cut and displayed his meat. Soon everyone was spending their money there. He was so shrewd, he could appraise any kind of beast at a glance, then convert it straightaway in his mind to cuts and joints, then to money.'

D'Nunzio finished his cappuccino and placed the cup back onto the saucer. 'Old Fabrizzio certainly prospered once, that's for sure,' he said.

'Another?' Andrea asked.

D'Nunzio looked at his watch. 'Why not.' He reached into his pocket.

'It's ok. Have it on the house.' Andrea held a fresh cup to the machine, filled it with steamy froth and pushed it towards him.

D'Nunzio took a couple of sips, then licked the froth from his upper lip.

Andrea wiped the bar. 'So Fabrizzio prospered once?'

D'Nunzio nodded his head, admiring his reflection in the mirror behind the bar. He tapped his pack of cigarettes on the counter again, then pulled another one out with his mouth, in the same exaggerated way and lit it. 'Yes,' he said. 'Until the babies came.'

Andrea looked away trying to keep his expression normal.

'The problems with his wife began after their first daughter was born,' he said. 'Living above the butcher's shop with nowhere else to go. Do you understand? There was her mother, but how often can you visit your mother? And she'd have to walk through the shop to get out onto the street, everyday past the meat. She said it bothered her, that she could sense the animals' spirits.' He gave another of his laughs. 'Then she stopped eating meat. Can you imagine that? Not eating meat!' He tapped the side of his head and shook it. 'After the second daughter, nobody saw her for months. Fabrizzio always said that she was fine and dismissed everyone with his stories. Then eventually she started going out again, always in new clothes and dark glasses, made up, like a film star, while her mother cared for the babies.' He stopped talking and drew on his cigarette. 'But where is there to go in this village? The main street, a few shops and the Piazza, from one to the other. Soon people began to tire of her. It wasn't a suitable example to set the younger women. Fabrizzio took it badly, there was talk, even though no indiscretions took place. Eventually he sent her to Rome. He had relatives there and the relatives knew a specialist. She came back from time to time, between treatments.'

'Treatments?' Andrea had to raise his voice to be heard above the men talking either side. 'What do you mean, treatments?'

D'Nunzio held his middle fingers either side of his head and tapped his temples. 'Electric shocks.' He mouthed the words exaggeratedly.

Andrea broke into to sweat.

'But they didn't do any good,' D'Nunzio continued. 'One time she showed up with a page she'd torn from a magazine. There was a picture of an old Greek vase that had been pieced back together from fragments. It was painted all the way round with people holding hands and dancing in a circle. She showed it to anyone who would pay attention, saying: "Look, once people held hands and danced together."' D'Nunzio became silent and his expression turned dumb with disbelief. 'She never set foot back in the butcher's shop after that. Her mother took to raising the infants, while Fabrizzio paid the expenses. Old Fabrizzio isn't the first man to be ruined by matrimony and I doubt if he will be the last.'

Some old men standing to one side laughed. Andrea thought they were laughing at him and turned towards them, then realised it was some joke that had passed between them. Their laughter filled the bar.

D'Nunzio held up his open palms. 'Do you know what the old fool did to raise money?' He was laughing, hardly able to contain himself.

Andrea wiped the coffee machine with his cloth, then pressed a lever and flushed steam around a pot for no particular reason. 'No,' he said. And shook his head.

D'Nunzio drew on his cigarette. 'People noticed straightaway, something about the meat had changed, the flavour and the colour, even the texture. The difference was slight, but people began to talk. In the end it was our old mayor that exposed him. He was from a farming family. He understood livestock. Do you understand?'

Andrea nodded despite understanding nothing about livestock.

'He was walking around the back of Fabrizzio's abattoir, saw the gate was ajar and walked in, on the pretext of saying good morning to the old man. He saw a cow's head resting on top of a bin full of entrails and suspected straight away, something to do with the size and shape of the horns. He went closer and curled back the creature's lips…It was fourteen years old! Something to do with the teeth gave it away. Then he looked through the window, into the cutting room and saw Fabrizzio in his apron, bent over slabs of meat, beating them with a mallet. The mallet had steel needles set in the face. A trick of the trade he'd no doubt learned in New York, to tenderize the meat. The very next day people stopped going to his shop. He never suspected a thing, no one ever told him, even to this day he hasn't realised it was our old mayor who tumbled him.' D'Nunzio stopped laughing. 'It's a mistake to take liberties with the village people. They're not as stupid as you might think.'

The saliva congealed in Andrea's throat. He swallowed, then looked through the window at Fabrizzio. He'd picked up his newspaper and sat hidden behind it.

One of D'Nunzio's friends stood up at his table out on the pavement. He tapped his watch and called out, 'Some of us have work to do you know.'

D'Nunzio stood up, put his cigarettes into his pocket and turned to leave.

'Wait,' Andrea called out. 'What happened to his wife?'

'A man from Accettura saved her.' He pointed to one of the villages up in the mountains a long way off. 'He was a former suitor, she turned him down when they were young, because he had no money, but he started to write when he heard of her predicament. Now they have some kind of a life together.'

He watched D'Nunzio cross the street, then cleared his cup and wiped the bar. He wiped it harder than he needed to, then he went around the other side of the bar and wiped the stool where D'Nunzio had been sitting.

The tables slowly emptied. Only Fabrizzio remained.

His daughter walked up. She took a letter out of her handbag without speaking and gave it to him. He fumbled with it for a while, then opened it. His face turned pale. After a couple of minutes, he stood up, searching his pockets. His daughter sighed and made a face, then reached into her handbag and laid some money on the table. She gave her father a long hard look, then turned and walked away. The old man fumbled through his pockets a little longer, then followed behind her. When they were out of sight Andrea cleared the table. The wine was finished and the Amoretti biscuits still lay in the saucer untouched. He went inside, locked the door and sat on one of the stools. The place was silent apart from an occasional hiss from the coffee machine. He lit a cigarette, inhaled a couple of times and sat staring through the window. The cigarette burnt down to a finger of ash in his hand without him noticing. He put it out, then washed the cups and saucers and all the ash-trays and dried everything ready for the evening. Then he put the stools up on the bar and swept the floor. He polished the coffee machine until it shone spotlessly, then he went upstairs to the apartment.

The place was quiet. The babies had to be asleep, maybe Lydia was sleeping too? Suddenly he wanted nothing more than to just watch over her, and the babies too. He opened the bedroom door carefully. Lydia was standing by the mirror putting on lipstick. She didn't speak, or acknowledge him, just pressed her lips together and gave a little pout, then she laid her jacket over her arm and walked to the door.

'Where are you going?' Andrea asked.

'The babies are asleep,' she said, 'I'm going out.'

The Jar of Pears

Mama unscrewed the top from the bottle and poured half the dye into a bucket. It lay in the water like a cloud of black smoke. I stirred it with a stick until it turned grey. She poured in the rest and it turned completely black, then she dropped in Papa's shirt. Air must've got trapped inside, because the material billowed up as though it was fighting for its life. She grabbed the stick from me and pushed it down until you could hardly see it under the water and swore. That was the first time I ever heard Mama swear.

I said, 'Mama, I don't get what all the fuss is about. Lots of men are wearing black shirts.' She gave me one of her - 'you're too young to understand' looks and poked it down even more.

Rafael started bawling. He'd hardly stopped all morning. Mama took him from his cradle and put him on her tit, rocking him all the time, then she undid herself and switched him to the other side.

'Maria Grazia,' she shouted. 'Go to Zia's house and get a jar of pears so we can have a salad tonight.'

Usually it was just plain Maria. It was late summer, and the larder was already full of pears. 'Yes, Mama,' I answered quickly before she could say, 'Take Dorotea with you' because I wanted to meet with Alfredo. Dorotea, or I should say Dummy, was standing in the corner sucking her thumb as usual. I guessed Mama didn't want me around, and it was a good time to go, because Matteo was playing happily for once, on the step with the top Papa had made him. Rafael did a big burp and threw up all over Mama, then lay back smiling. Mama took a breath and started cleaning herself up.

I poured some water onto my handkerchief to help her cool down. She winced and rubbed her belly. We usually washed our blood cloths out together, but she'd missed the last couple of times.

I said, 'Mama, you've got to take it easy if you're expecting another baby.'

Rafael started sucking again. She looked down at him as though that was answer enough. Just as I was going out the door she called out, 'Maria. Take Dorotea with you.'

We couldn't walk in the shade, because of the mules tethered to the houses either side. Dummy covered her ears and cried every time they eeawed. We had to step around their dung and when they peed it ran in streams between the cobbles.

'Look where you're going, Dummy.'

I couldn't understand why the men hadn't gone to work.

'And stop sucking your thumb.' She took it out of her mouth and sucked the shawl Mama used to wrap her in. She never let anyone take it from her, not even to wash. Ugh!

Zia's door was open and she was shouting. Zia used to be a quiet woman before Zio died. I waited a minute before calling out, 'Permesso,' and pushed through the streamers. Her house smelled of onions as usual, even though she wasn't cooking. Niccolo, my cousin, was chasing the hens around the house with a broom. It'd stop them laying for sure. One flew up onto the dresser, the other ran under the table. Niccolo crawled after it and came out the other side waving the broom. It flapped onto the bed and messed on the cover Zia had crocheted then perched up on the dresser too, looking down on us, squawking. Zia tried to catch Niccolo, but he dived back under the table and poked his head out the other side. He saw us and kept still, just long enough for her to grab him and smack his face. Dummy started blubbing. Niccolo stood there with his tongue hanging out, doing one of his ahuh ahuh laughs as though he were stupid... Mama says I must never say that... I took a handful of corn from the bin and made a trail with it into the coop. The hens peered over the edge of the dresser, fluffing up their feathers, then flew down scuffling over the corn until they were back inside. Zia shut the door, then grabbed the broom and beat Niccolo's backside, shrieking. She was red-faced and her hair hung down in tangles onto her long black mourning dress. He sat on the floor crying. I tried not to stare. Niccolo was sixteen, same as me, but much bigger, even bigger than Zio used to be. Zia turned away from us, pinning back her hair, then started stripping the bed. I'm sure she would've cried if we hadn't been there. It was going to be a big job, washing all that wool. I would've stayed to help, but she went off, then stood by the door with a jar of pears, I'd forgotten all about them and shoved a handful of figs into my pocket.

We walked the long way home past the church, to give Mama more time. Papa was there, taking up the marble floor, stacking it in piles on the bare dirt. The place was cool and smelled of earth and rows of painted angels, set into the ceiling either side, looked down on us. Two priests were talking to Papa up by the altar. Paolo, my brother, came in. His clothes were white and caked with lime. Some had got into his hair, turning it grey like Papa's.

I said, 'What's going on?' Papa and the priests turned and looked our way.

Paolo started playing with Dummy.

'What are those priests saying to Papa?'

'The new marble's been cancelled,' he whispered. 'There's no money. We've got to repair the old stuff.'

'Are they going to pay extra?'

Paolo didn't answer.

Papa bowed his head, as if he was being told off. I'd never seen him acting like that. The priests shook hands with him but didn't speak to us, just made the sign of the cross over our heads and left.

Papa's face was white like the marble and he wouldn't look at me. 'Where'd you get that jar of pears?' he asked.

'Zia gave them.'

He took Dummy and tickled her chin like he used to do with me.

'Matteo was spinning the top you made him when we left,' I said, hoping it would make him smile, which it did. 'And Rafael threw up over Mama.' He stopped tickling Dummy and stared at her. 'At least it stopped him blubbing,' I said, wondering if he knew about the new baby. They usually broke that kind of news to us over dinner; that's how it was with Dummy and Rafael, but come to think of it, they usually waited until she showed, just in case something happened. Papa kissed Dummy and passed her over to me. Then he kissed me too and started cleaning the marble.

The heat was making the mules dopey. Knots of flies clung to their faces as if they had a disease. Dummy held the shawl over her face because of the stink. There was a murmur of voices coming from the Piazza. It grew louder and echoed the closer we got, like dogs barking. Dummy got scared and started crying. 'Come on, Dummy.' I took her hand. Most of the men in the village were there, some were wearing black shirts and shouting. A couple of them started fighting. I got scared. Mama would've killed me if anything had happened to Dummy. Luckily Alfredo was there and came over. He'd dyed his shirt, or more likely his mother had, it looked good, because you couldn't see the darns and patches through the black dye. He seemed pleased with himself, older and more important looking. We walked back together as far as the barber shop. The door was locked and the shutters drawn. Everywhere had closed. We talked, while he made a fuss of

Dummy. Then he said goodbye and went off into the alley across the street, a short-cut; 'to meet a friend' was how he put it. I knew what he was thinking. It was a game we played whenever I had to look after Dummy. I hung around with her for a while, then gave her the jar of pears and told her to wait.

The alley was cool and dark and smelled of pee. Alfredo pressed me against the wall and put his hands inside my pants. I let him do it, even though I wasn't in the mood. He undid himself and I held it in my hand, but that wasn't what he wanted and pulled down my pants. He pushed it into me, shoving me against the wall. Dummy started bawling before he was done, then went quiet. I looked over his shoulder and saw her holding the jar of pears in her arms like a doll, watching us! Alfredo looked round. I felt him shrink then he took off up the alley. I pulled up my pants and got my breath. Dummy passed me the pears. I took them and smacked her face. Next thing I was hugging her to keep us both from blubbing.

When we got back, Matteo was sitting on the step, just as we'd left him, sulking.

'What is it, Matteo, broken your top?' I said, stepping over him.

He pulled it out of his pocket, good as new. 'Mama's not well,' he said, then his lip quivered. 'She told me to get Ermina.' Ermina was Mama's friend from school. Dummy looked as though she was going to start blubbing again, so I gave her and Matteo the figs Zia gave me and told them to wait.

Papa's shirt was hanging from the ceiling. Drops of black dye peppered the floor underneath. The bucket was in the corner with a towel draped over it. I lifted the towel and saw Mama's blood-stained underwear soaking. Then the heat hit me. The stove was blazing even though it wasn't mealtime and there was a parcel in the flames, tied tight with string. It caught, then burst open and I saw a tiny frog inside, covered with slime.

'Maria Grazia!' Ermina had come from Mama's bedroom.

'Your Mama's resting,' she said, standing in front so I wouldn't see. The fire hissed and Ermina held my hand. When the blaze died down she took me to Mama's room. Mama was sleeping peacefully with Rafael next to her.

'Sit with your Mama while I make some broth,' Ermina said, picking up her bag. 'And let me take those pears.'

I'd forgotten all about them.

The sheet was moving up and down, in time with Mama's breathing. I wanted badly to wake her up. I wanted to talk to her.

The Thrush

Vito's mother was washing a bedsheet. The wet linen hung over the edge of the trough, slopping soapy water onto the street.

'He'll be company for his grandfather' Vito's father said.

Vito's mother stopped scrubbing and put down the bar of soap, which was the same size and shape as a house brick. She dried her hands on her apron, then brought the apron up and dried the sweat from her face.

'Vito needs to go to school,' she said.

'But he may be able to convince your father to move back to the village,' Vito's father replied.

'It's impossible to convince my father to do anything!' She spat on the ground. Then she gathered the sheet up into the water and pushed it under, working it with her hands, as though she were trying to drown it.

'It'll be one less mouth to feed,' he said, undeterred.

She pulled out the plug. The water sluiced out onto the street and ran away between the cobbles. Then she replaced the plug and cranked the rusty pump harder than ever and continued her work.

The thrush stopped singing and looked around as though it were being watched. Then it flew down and scratched at the dry earth around the almond trees. Vito had seen the thrush a couple of times before. He liked its shape and the colour of its feathers. He especially liked the sound of its singing. Yesterday he told his grandfather about it. His grandfather said that birds were often very beautiful and their songs could be beautiful too.

Then his grandfather said: 'But you can't eat songs. It's good to eat meat when you can get it and a thrush would make a good broth.'

The thrush flew out of sight. Vito walked back to his grandfather's house, stopping every few minutes to look up at the village. White-washed houses, sprawled over the mountain top, were reflecting the sun. He wondered what his mother and father were doing and if they still thought about him.

His grandfather was sitting outside the door snoring, with a hoe lying across his lap. Vito walked around him into the house and lay down on his bed. His grandfather's bed was shoved against the wall opposite. There was a table between them, with some tomatoes lying randomly on it. One of them had started to rot and a knot of flies were fighting noisily over the putrid moisture.

Vito stared past the table-legs and noticed, for the first time, a tangle of iron and chains under his grandfather's bed.

He got up, pulled it out and began examining it. Just as he was unwinding the chain, the door opened behind him and a wedge of sunshine lit up the dull room. Vito turned around and saw his grandfather silhouetted in the doorway. The old man stumbled in, clutching the upturned hoe as if it were a staff.

Vito tried to push the tangle of metal back under the bed without his grandfather seeing but it screeched against the brick floor, making Vito wince.

The old man heard and stared at it curiously, then he poked it with the handle of his hoe.

Vito looked up at him, uncertain whether or not to feel guilty.

'What's that?' the old man asked.

'Your old boar-trap.'

The old man shook his head, then poked it again. 'Spread it out, will you?'

Vito unrolled the chain. There was a long iron stake fixed to one end. The top was flattened over from frequent hammering and the other end had been worked into a sharp point.

'What's that?' He tapped the foot-plate with the end of his hoe.

'The jaws.' Vito pressed down with his foot and tried to pull them apart, but he wasn't strong enough. 'That's where the boar steps,' he said. 'Then the jaws clamp around its leg. You caught a boar with it once and brought it back to the village on your mule. Its jaws were this big!' Vito opened his arms. 'And it had a gash in its neck, like a gill, where you struck it with your axe. Blood dripped from it onto the ground! Don't you remember?'

The old man shook his head. 'No, I don't…What about that thrush?' he said eventually. 'Have you caught it yet?'

'No… Not yet.'

Vito's sheet was soaked with sweat. His grandfather was across the room, snoring. His hoe had fallen off the bed and was lying across the floor. Vito woke up first and took the sheet outside, drying his face on it as he walked, then draped it over an olive bough. He went to the well and stared at his reflection in the water as he did every morning. Then he let the bucket fall. A couple of moments passed and his reflection turned into ripples. He hauled up the bucket hand over hand and washed himself. When he'd stopped shivering, he drew another bucket and left it by the door. Then he went off searching, uncertain of what for, until he was standing among some rows of withering sweet-corn stems. He started pulling up the tallest ones until a pile formed. That done, he chopped the roots off on a block with a bill-hook, then trimmed their ends until they were the same length and wove them into a screen the same height as himself. He held the screen vertically, then let it fall. It descended slowly, as if in slow motion, then made a shushing sound as it hit the ground. He carried it to the almond grove where he'd seen the thrush and propped it up with a stick.

Then he kicked the stick away sharply. The screen fell again, much faster.

The following day, Vito dropped the bucket into the well without bothering to stare at his reflection. After washing quickly and leaving the full bucket by the door, he went around to the back of the shack where it was shady and began turning over the old, discarded roof tiles that his grandfather stored there. Frogs hopped from beneath them, leaving behind knots of snails. Their brown and yellow-striped shells reminded him of the sweets his mother made at Christmas. He filled both his pockets with snails, then went around to the front of the shack where his grandfather usually sat. The bucket hadn't been touched. Vito pushed the door until it was ajar and heard his grandfather snoring.

There was a ball of twine, wound around a length of wood, pushed up under the eaves. Vito took it down and began unwinding it, then, uncertain of how much he'd need, he rolled it back up and took it with him to the almond grove.

He tied one end of the twine to the stick holding up his screen and unwound the rest, as if he were laying a fuse. He stopped at a gorse bush covered with yellow flowers and took cover behind it, then pulled the twine sharply. A moment later the screen fell silently to the ground. He walked over to it, smiling, and propped it back up. Then he took the snails from his pockets and scattered them under the screen, as if he were casting dice. After studying them carefully, he returned to the cover of the gorse bush and waited.

It was hot and Vito soon became bored. There was no sign of the thrush, or any other birds for that matter. He put it down to the heat and decided to get up even earlier the next day, or maybe come back in the evening. He began rolling up the twine. About a quarter of the way through, he decided this was a waste of time because his grandfather never used the twine. He unrolled it back to the gorse bush. Then he saw a thrush, close to but not under the screen. It was beating a snail against a rock with its beak. It pecked through the shell and swallowed the snail greedily. When it was done, it took cover in an almond tree and perched there, looking content, turning its head gently from side to side, studying the ground. Eventually it flew down again and began pecking at another snail, also close to but not under the screen. After it had eaten the snail, it flew off.

Vito walked over to the screen and stared at the iridescent slime trails that the snails had left behind. He searched and found a couple of snails which he put back in his pocket. Then he stared at the sky in the direction the thrush had taken and scratched his head.

It was close to noon when Vito approached the shack. His grandfather was shouting and throwing objects around. Vito knocked, then tentatively opened the door. The old man was standing in the middle of the room with his back to him, beating the end of his hoe against the floor. The beds were turned over onto their sides, the boar trap with the chain unwound lay strewn over the floor between them. Nothing was in its usual place.

The old man turned around: 'I can't remember where I've put it,' he shouted. He was wearing his shirt inside out and buttoned irregularly, so that the side of the collar rode up level with his ear.

'Where you put what, Grandfather?' Vito asked.

'The twine. Do you know where it is?' He lurched around the room, poking his hoe into the corners.

'No…But I can help you look for it.'

Vito walked over towards him. 'First let me help you with your shirt.'

The old man flailed out with his free hand.

Vito winced and put his hand up to his mouth.

'Did I do that?' The old man asked, pointing at Vito's bleeding mouth.

'No.' Vito said, sucking his lip... 'It was an accident. Now let me help you with your shirt?'

The old man fumbled with the buttons, then gave up.

The next morning, Vito got up before it was fully light and washed himself, then he refilled the bucket and took it into the shack. He woke his grandfather then helped him wash and dress.

Then he peeled the cloth from around a loaf of bread and examined it. The bread was hard and free from mould. He sawed through it on the table-top, poured some olive oil onto a plate, then dropped the slice into it. After about a minute, he turned the slice of bread over, selected a tomato from the pile and crushed it over the bread.

'Come and sit down,' Vito said, breaking the silence that had formed between them.

The old man came over, tapping the ground with his hoe. He sprinkled salt and oregano from a pot onto his bread, then looked over at Vito's swollen lip and started crying.

'It's alright,' Vito said… 'It was an accident.'

The old man bit into the bread and worked it around his mouth, then swallowed it with much effort. 'I wish I could remember where I put the twine,' he said. 'The vines are trailing on the ground. If it rains, they'll be lying in mud.'

'Maybe you left it there the last time you tied them.' Vito said.

The old man stared at him.

Vito couldn't bear it and looked away. He sawed through the bread again, preparing himself a slice.

'No,' the old man replied. 'I always bring it back and hang it up there.' He pointed to the place under the eaves and stared. 'Do you know what day it is?'

'Sunday,' Vito replied. He took a bite from his bread and worked it around his mouth.

'That's good. Your Zia will be here later with some fresh bread.' The old man chewed another mouthful and shook his head. 'Hope she brings some meat!'

Vito's face broke into a smile. The sun was filtering through the cobwebs, covering the tiny window. 'Yes. And we can gather her some figs. The ones against the south wall are ripe.'

'And shell some almonds from the barrel.' The old man was smiling too. 'And talking of meat. Have you caught that thrush yet?'

'No…not yet.'

The sky was blue and free of clouds. It was going to be hot.

'Look, up there above your head,' the old man shouted and pointed with his hoe. He was holding up a basket.

Vito picked a couple of figs then dropped them into the basket. 'Do we have enough yet?'

'Yes. More than enough. There'll be enough for your mother too!'

Vito climbed down.

The old man took a couple of figs and gave one to Vito.

Another smile broke over Vito's face. 'How long before Zia gets here?' He chewed his fig and swallowed it.

'If she went to the early Mass - which knowing your Zia, she did - then leaves straightaway…around midday, I'd say.'

'Why do Zia and Zio always come and not my mother and father?' Vito asked.

'Because Zia doesn't have any children.'

'Why doesn't Zia have any children?'

'Well…They keep trying, but they just don't come,' the old man replied.

'How do they try?' Vito asked. 'And why don't they come?'

The old man looked away and began scratching marks in the ground with his hoe.

'How do they try, Grandfather?' Vito repeated. 'And why don't they come?'

The old man looked down at the marks he'd made, as if an answer were lying there among them. 'You must've seen the goats around the village,' he said eventually. 'And the dogs!'

Vito recollected the goats and dogs. He thought of his mother and father! His face reddened.

'I still don't understand,' he said. 'What is it they do?'

The old man scratched more marks with his hoe… 'I don't know,' he said, shaking his head. 'Ask your father when you see him… And what about the twine, have you found it yet?'

'No… Not yet. I'll go and search among the vines. You probably left it there the last time you tied them.'

As soon as Vito was out of sight, he took a detour to the grove.

Ants were scurrying over the ground beneath the screen where his snails had been. He kicked away the stick and began rolling up the twine. When he reached the gorse bush, he kicked that too. Pinpricks of blood rose to the surface of his shin. He bent over and massaged it. Eventually the pain subsided and he stared at the gorse bush, touching it tentatively with his palm. He tried pulling off a thorny branch but it pricked his fingers. Then he realized there were fewer thorns at the base of each branch. He pulled carefully at them until a pile formed, then he took off his shirt, spread it over the ground and pushed the pile of gorse onto it with his boot and carried it carefully to his screen.

He propped it up again. The ground over which it had lain was still covered with iridescent snail trails. He arranged the strands of gorse in a circle around them to form a thorny wall.

Then he took the last two remaining snails from his pocket and dropped them in. The snails emerged eventually and began exploring with their antennae extended until they reached the gorse walls, then retreated back into their shells. Vito smiled to himself, then looked up at the village, raising his hand to ward off the sun. People were slowly descending the hairpin bends in groups or pairs. Some were leading donkeys. He tried to identify his Zia and Zio but they were too far away, like insects. He put the two snails back in his pocket and went back to the shady place at the rear of the shack to search for more. He filled his pockets until they bulged. His grandfather was inside making tapping sounds.

Vito opened the door and saw him bent over the table with a hammer in his hand, cracking almonds and putting them in a bowl. A mound of empty shells lay by his feet.

The old man looked up. 'Did you find the twine?' he asked.

'No... Not yet. I searched through the vines but they're so overgrown it could easily have got covered over. I'll go again this evening, when it's cooler.'

The old man stared at him. 'I don't know what I'm going to do. I always I put it up there,' he said, pointing with his hammer up at the eaves.

Vito cleared the almond shells and took them outside.

Zia became slowly visible at the end of the track, riding a donkey half her size. Its legs were buckling under her weight. Zio, a tall, matchstick-looking man, under a broad-rimmed straw hat, held the rein and walked in front.

Vito tried to imagine them making a baby.

The old man came out, saw the puzzled expression on Vito's face and scratched the earth with his hoe again, as if he knew what Vito was thinking.

They were still standing on the same spot when Zia eventually arrived and slid off the donkey's back. She looked around, anxiously running her hands up and down her long, black dress.

When it was smoothed to her satisfaction, she began twisting her wedding ring around her finger.

Then she saw Vito's swollen lip.

'What's happened to you?' She shouted, throwing her hands into the air.

The old man looked down at the ground.

'It was an accident,' Vito said quickly... 'I wasn't looking where I was going and walked into the door.'

Zia looked at them both in turn. She touched Vito's chin. He looked up and she examined his lip.

'What would your Mother say?' Zia said, then she kissed him on both cheeks and hugged him so hard his feet left the ground.

A crunching sound came from Vito's pockets. He stepped back, catching his breath.

'Have you got eggs in your pockets!?' Zia asked.

Vito shook his head.

'Then what?' She pushed her hands into Vito's pockets and pulled them out again. 'Ugh!... Snails!' She cried. 'What have you been teaching him! Ugh...' She cried again, holding up her slime-covered hands.

The old man covered his ears.

Zio pulled down the brim of his hat and looked away.

'I've been collecting snails,' Vito said… 'There's nothing else to do around here!'

Zia calmed and noticed the basket of figs Vito was still managing to hold. She took them from him, then kissed him again, just once.

Zio untied a net from the donkey's saddle. 'I'm going down to the river,' he said. He shook the old man and Vito by the hand and hobbled the donkey's feet.

'Why don't you ride to the river?' the old man asked.

'The donkey's exhausted,' Zio replied.

All three of them looked at Zia.

Zia smoothed her hands up and down her dress again.

Zio touched the rim of his hat and walked off.

'I've got something for you,' Zia said. Then she unhooked a bag from the donkey's saddle, took out a parcel and gave it to Vito. 'From your mother. She made them last night.'

Vito unfolded a corner. 'Almond biscuits!'

Both their faces broke into smiles.

'And this is for you,' she said, coldly, handing her father a blood-stained parcel.

He unwrapped it and held up a goat's neck, stripped of flesh.

'When you catch that thrush, Vito,' he said, examining the bones. 'Then we'll have a real broth.'

'Catching thrushes! What have you been teaching him!' Zia shouted. 'As if collecting snails wasn't enough! If you moved back to the village, Vito could go back to school. He could learn something useful!'

Zia marched into the shack, still shouting, then came out again with their wicker chairs. She brushed them down, then went back inside and threw their used bedding out the door.

Vito moved the chairs into the lean-to wood-store, next to the shack. Shards of sunlight broke through where the tiles were broken and lit up patches on the ground. The old man's axe was lying discarded in the dirt. Vito picked it up and tried to swing it but it was too heavy.

'What are you going to do when the snow comes?' Vito asked.

'We'll gather some wood before then.' The old man took his axe and examined it. 'It just needs sharpening,' he muttered.

'Why don't you move back to the village?' he asked.

The old man didn't answer.

Zia called them in.

The floor was swept, everything was clean and the cobwebs removed from the window.

Vito brought in the chairs and put them back either side of the table. An iron pot hanging over the fire bubbled, and onion smells filled the room.

Zia brought the pot to the table, ladled out a pile of bones into two bowls, then covered them with pale liquid.

Vito sat down opposite his grandfather, leaning his elbows on the clean tablecloth Zia had brought.

Zia twisted her wedding ring around her finger.

'Aren't you having any?' her father asked.

'I'll wait until evening.' She smoothed her hands down her dress, then rested them, one inside the other, over her waist. 'Give me your shirt, Vito,' she said suddenly.

Vito put his spoon down.

'Look at this button. It's about to fall off.'

Vito stood up and removed his shirt.

Zia stared at his ribs and gave her father a look. Then she took a needle and thread from under her collar and quickly sowed back the button.

Vito put his shirt back on then resumed sucking a bone.

The old man prized a tangle of bones apart with his fingers and laid them on the table-cloth. Then he selected one and worked it noisily around his mouth.

'When were you last in the village, Vito?' Zia asked

Vito put the sucked bone on the edge of his bowl. 'Six weeks ago.'

'Six weeks!'

The old man looked up at her for a moment, then let a bone fall from his mouth into his bowl. Some onion-coloured liquid splashed onto the tablecloth.

'At least if Vito lived at the village,' Zia said, 'he could help his father and learn something useful, instead of collecting snails. Ugh!'

The old man removed a bone from his mouth, examined it carefully, then put it back and continued sucking it noisily.

'So, Vito, you've missed Mass for six weeks too?' she said.

Vito nodded.

'Every Sunday the priest asks: "Where's Vito?" What am I supposed to tell him?'

The old man leaned away from the table, opened his mouth and let the bone fall onto the floor.

Vito and Zia pretended not to notice.

'What are we supposed to do if something happens to you?' she asked. 'It'll take Vito at least two hours to get back to the village, even if he runs all the way.' She wiped her eyes on her sleeve.

The old man leaned away from the table again, opened his mouth and let another bone fall onto the floor.

'Then we have to find the doctor,' Zia continued. 'If he's free it will take at least another two hours to get to you!'

The old man took another bone from the tablecloth and sucked it noisily. Some grease ran down his chin. He leaned forward, wiped his chin on the tablecloth and let the bone fall from his mouth.

Vito looked down at the pile of bones on the floor, then he looked at Zia.

The old man worked his way meticulously through the remaining bones until they were all sucked clean and lying on the floor. He looked down at them then up at his daughter and nodded.

Zia screwed up her face, as if she were a little girl, then pulled a handkerchief from her sleeve and went outside.

The old man smiled at Vito, then stared into space.

Vito heard Zia and Zio talking and went outside. They were facing each other with their heads bowed. Zio's net was lying on the wet ground, bulging and convulsing.

Vito filled the bucket at the well and brought it over.

Zio tipped his net into it. A tangle of eels thrashed around, stirring the water into a froth.

Zio stood upright smiling proudly.

Zia looked up at him and smiled too.

'Do you have another bucket, Vito?' she asked.

Vito fetched it and filled it with water.

Zia pulled out a tangle of squirming eels with her hand and dropped them into the bucket.

'You can relight the fire and roast them tonight,' she said.

Zio loaded the donkey.

Zia bent down and kissed Vito.

Vito watched them disappearing along the track. The bucket of eels was making Zio lean over to one side. Zia leaned into his other side and the donkey followed behind.

Vito brought his grandfather outside, settled him into his chair and went back inside. The fire had burned down to a few red embers. He raked ash over them, then, satisfied with their suffocation, returned to his grandfather. The old man was snoring. Vito went around to the back of the shack and searched under the tiles for more snails. He gathered a pocketful, then went to the almond grove.

The twine lay stretched over the ground, just as he'd left it. He decided that he'd lied enough and would return it at the end of the day, whether he'd caught the thrush or not. He positioned the screen and propped it up with the stick. Then he emptied his pocket, tossing the snails randomly onto the ground inside the prickly perimeter, as if he were sowing seeds.

Then he followed the twine back to the gorse bush and took cover behind it. He looked up at the sky. Sweat ran down his forehead into his eyes. He wiped them with his hands. Then he looked back at his screen and saw two thrushes fighting over a snail. He pulled the twine sharply. The screen fell, then heaved up and down as the thrushes continued to fight. He sprinted toward them, then threw himself headlong, placing one hand on top of the screen, while sliding the other one underneath until he had both birds in his grip. He pulled them out. They pecked his fingers and flapped. Some feathers floated to the ground. Then he beat their heads against a rock and felt their final throes and spasms until eventually their heads fell back motionless.

Vito shook his grandfather's shoulder gently to wake him, holding up the thrushes for him to see. His knees were grazed from his dive and the roll of twine was tucked under his arm.

'You caught the thrush!' his grandfather said, sitting himself up in his chair.

'Yes. Two of them! And look, I found the twine!'

'The twine….' He took it from him and examined it. 'I didn't know it was lost.'

Mathematics
(part one)

Giovanino woke up in the half-light. Matilda, the family's ass, was scuffling noisily in her stall below him. She raised her tail and urinated. He propped his elbow on the pillow, listening to the splashing, and watched the steaming liquid flow over the brick floor, into the cracks in between and out under the door to the street outside. The sight made his own bladder tighten. He got up, reached quietly for the metal bucket under his bed and urinated also, directing the flow carefully against the side of the pail to dull the sound. Giovanino didn't want to attract his mother's attention and be called down. He peered through a hole in the tattered curtain that divided his bed and the mezzanine floor from the main room of the house below. His mother was stooping in front of the hearth, raking the cinders with a stick. She held Filomena, his baby sister, in the crook of her arm. Filomena sucked quietly at her breast. On the floor clutching his mother's leg was another sister, Rosina. Rosina pushed up the long black skirt and pressed her face against her mother's warm thigh. The skirt rested on her head and hung down either side of her face like a nun's habit. His mother bent down onto one knee, dropped a twig onto the embers and began blowing. A flame caught and she added more twigs until a fire established itself, then she hung a blackened kettle from the hook above the fire. The smell of wood-smoke began to fill the house, all the way up to the vaulted ceiling and into the loft, where Giovannino was now sitting on the edge of his bed. He reached under his pillow, took out his slate and chalk and began to draw columns of numbers, which he added and subtracted. His mind worked out the answers in seconds, which he then scribbled at the foot of the slate. Then he erased it all with some spit and the palm of his hand and quickly began again, with complicated multiplication and long division, over and over. Numbers fascinated Giovannino, the patterns and relationships between them were as apparent to him as the fingers on his hands. Some people said he had a gift, others said it was an affliction, like his epilepsy.

Father Pasquale said that God touched people in whatever way He saw fit and that it wasn't acceptable for ordinary people to question His reasons.

Giovannino's father got up from his bed, dressed and sat upright in his chair.

'Fucking influenza,' he muttered, then hawked noisily from the back of his throat and sent a ball of gob hissing into the fire. He looked at the empty recess beside the hearth where the fired wood was stored and shook his head.

'Giov-a-nino,' his mother called as though she were singing his name.

Giovannino pushed back the tattered curtain and looked down. 'Mama,' he shouted. 'Today Professor Lombardi is going to teach me algebra!'

'Not today Giovannino. You have things to do. Perhaps tomorrow.'

'But Mama.'

His father coughed and for a moment everyone in the house was silent.

His mother winced, then slid her little finger into Filomena's mouth, prizing the child's new milk teeth from around her nipple, then she cradled her head.

'What are you dreaming about, little one?' she said and laid her into the crib.

Rosina raised her arms and clasped her hands around her mother's neck, replacing Filomena in a moment.

'Gra-zi-ella,' his mother called, as if singing once again.

Graziella, Giovannino's third sister pushed back the curtain that separated her bed from Goivannino's and peered down.

'I can't go to school today, Mama,' she called. 'I've got a headache.' Then she pulled a tangle of long black hair over her face to cover her grin.

'It's not fair,' Giovannino shouted. 'Graziella never wants to go to school but I'm doing algebra today with Professor Lombardi.'

His father cleared his throat again and spat rudely into the fire.

Giovannino picked up his bucket quietly and carried it carefully down the ladder and opened the door. The new day's light flooded into the house freshening the night's stale smells. He tipped the pail of urine into the gutter, then cleared the balls of dung that had collected around Matilda's hind legs with a broom and added them to the pile beside the door.

'Oofah,' he said, patting Matilda's neck. Then he unfastened her lead-rein and ushered her backwards through the door. Matilda stamped her hooves on the cobbles and made blowing sounds through her nostrils. 'Oofah,' he said again. Then tethered her tightly to the wall.

His mother untangled Rosina's arms from around her neck and placed her back on the floor, where she immediately clamped her arms around her warm thigh once more. She walked to the table dragging the child along like a leech, then unwrapped a great slab of bread from a moist cloth; she held it to her chest and began slicing, turning the slab just before the knife touched her neck as though it were some kind of a dance, until half the loaf lay in a pile of long, oval slices on the table.

'How long has it been since Giovanino's last fit?' his father asked.

'Two months, one week and three days,' she replied.

'And before that?'

'Two months, three weeks and four days.'

'It must be you he gets his mathematics from,' he said, shaking his head. 'And before that?'

'Four months two weeks and three days.'

'Hum… Do you think he's up to going to the forest to fetch firewood?'

'If God goes with him,' she replied. Then she kissed the tips of her fingers, touched the wooden crucifix that hung on the wall and crossed herself.

Giovanino came back inside. He selected the ripest tomato from the pile on the table, crushed it onto a piece of bread with his palm and ate it. 'Papa,' he said. 'Today Professor Lombardi is going to teach me algebra.'

His father shook his head and looked down at the meagre flame warming the blackened kettle, then turned to the empty space beside the hearth where the firewood was stored. 'Tell me,' he said. 'What is this algebra? I went to school until I was your age, I never heard anything about any algebra.' He leaned forward in his chair and held up his opened palms. 'Answer me this question. How will algebra fill your belly? Huh?' He raised his eyebrows into an arch. 'Can you tell me that, and will your algebra fetch your mother's firewood?'

'But Papa, Professor Lombardi says that algebra is another way of discovering things. He says that last year mathematicians went to South America during an eclipse and made pictures. Do you know what an eclipse is?' He held up his hands to demonstrate the position of the sun and moon and their movement past each other. 'Professor Lombardi says that a man called Albert Einstein has worked out that light is bent by gravity! And he's worked out the speed of light, with algebra! That's what you can do with algebra, Papa. Albert Einstein says that if you travel faster than the speed of light, time goes backwards and you become younger!' Giovanino began to smile and his eyes glowed excitedly.

His father stared at him in incomprehension, then he reached into his pocket and pulled out a tiny, misshapen potato; he cut it in half and placed it in his tobacco pouch to maintain the moisture. Then he rolled himself a cigarette and lit it. The end flared for a moment. He inhaled a couple of times, coughed, then put the cigarette out and placed it behind his ear.

'I've got something for you,' he said. And smiled. 'A present.' He pushed down on the arms of his chair until he was standing upright and took a paper parcel from beneath the bed.

Giovanino opened it carefully and held up a greasy cap and a pair of long trousers that had been patched so often that little of the original trousers remained.

'They were your cousin, Calogero's,' his father said proudly. 'And before that his brother Donato's, all the brothers, Pietro, Cenzino, Peppino, Domenico, Tonino, they've all worn them. There won't be any more sons now that your aunt has turned fifty and now, they're yours.' He continued to smile. 'Go on, put them on.'

Giovannino took off his shorts and put on the trousers.

'Roll them up,' his father said. He took the flapping waistband and tied it tightly round his son's waist with some twine. He studied him carefully, smoothing the patched fabric with the palm of his hand, then placed the cap roughly on Giovannino's head.

'There, no one would think you were only eight years old. Today you've become a man,' he said and sat back in his chair.

Giovannino's mother tipped the kettle from its hook and poured hot water onto some ground, roast barley and placed it before her husband. He pushed the steaming cup away without speaking. She took a bottle of wine and a chipped and stained glass from a cupboard. He poured for himself and drank, then wiped his mouth on the back of his hand. The smell of hot, roast barley and wine began to fill the house.

Graziella climbed down the ladder. 'What's for breakfast mama?'

'What did you have for breakfast yesterday?'

'Bread and tomato.'

'And the day before that?'

'Bread and tomato.'

'And what do you think you'll be having for breakfast today?'

She screwed up her pretty brown face. 'Bread and tomato?'

'Yes, you guessed it,' her mother said. And crushed a tomato onto some bread and sprinkled it with salt and oregano from a pot and a few spits of olive oil. Then she kissed Graziella's forehead and gave the hot barley drink to Giovannino. He took it outside so that no one would see his tears.

'Giovannino, come here and help me with this.' His father staggered outside, panting, with Matilda's saddle in his arms. He threw it onto the ass's back and leaned against her, then spat onto the ground. 'Quickly do up her belly strap,' he shouted.

Giovannino threaded the leather strap through the buckle and pulled it tight.

'Not like that. Like this.' His father brought his knee up into Matilda's stomach. She winced and inhaled sharply. He pulled the

53

strap hard and tightened it a couple more notches. 'Don't let her make a fool of you,' he said, tapping the side of his forehead with his finger. 'Donkeys are crafty animals. If she gives you any trouble then show her this.' He clenched his fist and held it against her muzzle. Matilda stood obediently, then shuffled her hooves, making clicking sounds on the cobbles.

He went back inside and fetched a bill-hook. 'Now this is for cutting side branches,' he said. It had a wooden handle, smooth and polished through use, and a blade that curled at the end into a hook. 'You sharpen it like this.' He spat onto the blade and rubbed a stone over it, round and round until he reached the end, then turned it over and worked the other side. The blackened metal turned silver along its edge and began to shine. 'You try.'

Giovannino began copying his father. The sound of the stone on the metal hurt his ears. He thought of Professor Lombardi waiting for him in class. 'I'll work hard today papa,' he said. 'Then tomorrow I'll go to school,'

His father went back into the house again without replying and returned with a larger axe.

Giovannino took hold of its curved handle; he felt the uneven balance of the blade, top heavy as though its weight alone would split a log, and worked the stone over its curved edge until it turned into a shiny, silver smile.

'That's for cutting the thicker wood. Cut it into lengths like this,' his father said. He held his arms out wide. 'Load the heavy wood evenly, either side of her saddle. Mostly oak if you can find it. It will season for winter. Then pile the dry twigs on top, so your mother will be able to cook tonight. Pile it as high as you can. Matilda will complain. It's a female's place to complain but don't let her make a fool of you. It will take you two hours to reach the forest, so don't come back half-loaded.'

His wife appeared at the door with his chair and placed it against the wall, facing the early morning sunshine. He sat down, took the partly smoked cigarette from behind his ear and lit it again.

'Zio Nicole will be along soon. You can walk with him as far as the bridge with the flaming olive tree, then he will go to his land and you can go on to the forest.'

Giovannino's mother reappeared with some food wrapped in a cloth. She gave it to him, then turned her back on her husband and leaned over Giovannino and kissed him, holding his face in her hands. 'I'm sorry you can't go to school today,' she whispered.

'Tomorrow Mama, after I've fetched the firewood,' he whispered back.

She looked up at the sky, then at her husband and shook her head. 'Tomorrow? Who knows what tomorrow will bring?' she said. 'Only God knows.'

The sound of hooves clicking on the cobbles preceded Zio Nicole by a few seconds, then he arrived leading a young, skittish mule with a ploughshare tied to its saddle. The mule shook its head and stamped its hooves on the cobbles exaggeratedly, like a petulant child. Matilda looked up sulkily from beneath her eyelids, as though she knew she would have to trot fast to keep up.

Zio Nicole touched the side of his forehead and exchanged looks with Giovanino's father.

His father shrugged his shoulders. 'Fucking epilepsy,' he muttered.

Giovanino looked around and kicked at the cobbles awkwardly.

His mother reappeared with Rosina still attached to her leg and Filomena in the crook of her arm. She stroked Graziela's hair with her free hand.

His father raised his hand and pointed a finger at Giovanino. 'You must understand that we are lucky people,' he said. 'We have a piece of land down by the river and a donkey to work for us. Where would we be without our land and Matilda?'

Giovanino nodded, then untied Matilda's lead rein and followed his uncle down the narrow street.

The village was built on three hills. Giovanino lived in the highest part. They descended the first maze of narrow streets. A goat tethered to the wall at one side bleated dumbly, next to where a young woman sat in an open doorway nursing her baby. Then the street opened into a small Piazza. A group of women and a young girl filled clay pitchers from a pump. Matilda and the mule sank their muzzles into the trough making whispering sounds as they drank. Zio Nicole cupped his hands into the water beside them and washed his face, then pressed a finger against each nostril in turn and blew snot out onto the ground. Giovanino did the same. Roof tops stretched out below them, then the land dropped down to the valley. The Basento followed the contours of the partly dried-up riverbed. And a train, invisible from the village, stood in the station, puffing smoke into the blue sky. The smoke rose up vertically, thick and black, hardly dispersing in the still air. Giovanino cupped his hand above his eyes to stop the glare and stared across the valley to Calciano, a patch of white perched at the top of a bare hill, like a mirror reflecting back his own village. His mother once told him that Calciano was identical to their own village in every way and that every time he looked across to it, a little boy exactly like him, with the same name and thoughts, would be staring back.

A young girl rested her pitcher on the trough. 'Are you thinking of going to Calciano to find yourself a bride?' she shouted.

The women started to laugh, then they became quiet and exchanged looks with one another. Giovanino had not yet realized that his epilepsy would make him an unwelcome suitor to any of the families in his village. He stared at the clay pitchers, confused, then began to notice for the first time how they rose from their narrow bases and broadened like the hips of women, then narrowed again into their necks, where the handles curved out either side, like tiny arms. The women finished filling their pitchers, then, silent as nuns, placed them on their heads and walked off down the street in their long, black, bell-shaped dresses.

Giovanino, with his head bowed, following the sweep of the mule's tail, walked to the lower part of the village. The square cobbles there were set in concentric circles, then splayed out into sweeping curves. Giovanino began to think about circles and curves and wondered if at some point a curve became a straight line and that perhaps a straight line was really a long, shallow curve but that no one really knew. Then he thought, perhaps a straight line might be part of a circle and if you followed it you would arrive back at the point you started.

'Zio Nicole,' he shouted. 'Do you think a straight line could be part of a circle?'

'Save your energy for walking.' His uncle shouted back without turning his head and pulled roughly at his mule's rein. 'Straight lines and circles won't fill your belly.'

They passed Professor Lombardi's house. The shutters were still closed tight to keep out the early morning light. 'I'll ask Professor Lombardi at school tomorrow,' Giovanino thought. The cobbles gave way to the road and the sound of clip-clopping became a dull scrape. The train began to move out of the station and eased its way slowly out of the valley. Giovanino followed the trail of black smoke, then broke into a run with Matilda following behind, until he was walking alongside Zio Nicole.

'Where is the train going?' he asked.

'To Bari or Napoli.' Beads of sweat began to appear on Zio Nicole's face; he wiped them off with the back of his hand.

'What is it like at those places?'

'They're ports and the sea is there.'

'What does the sea look like?'

Zio Nicole yawned and stretched his arms. 'The sea is big and deep,' he said. 'It's made of blue salt water and you can't see across to the other side. Great ships sail on it to other countries, America for instance.'

'How big are these ships?'

'Very big,' he said, nodding his head.

'As big as a house?'

Zio Nicole shook his head. 'No, as big as lots of houses put together.'

'As big as the village?'

Zio Nicole stopped and looked back up to the village; he took off his cap and scratched his head as though working out a difficult calculation, then shrugged his shoulders and shook his head uncertainly. 'Perhaps as big as the village. People sleep on them in cabins.' He wiped more sweat from his face. Giovanino did the same.

'When did you see the ships?' Giovanino asked.

Zio Nicole's mule stood still and refused to go any further. He slapped its face, then pulled its rein and strutted off down the road without answering. Giovanino broke into another run until he was walking alongside again.

'When did you see them, Zio Nicole?'

Zio Nicole looked away and his face turned red. 'I haven't seen them… But my wife's brother in law has seen them,' he said quickly. 'He's been to America, to Brooklyn, New York City'. He repeated the words again, then held his head up as though he had just said something very important. They turned the first hairpin bend and the village disappeared from sight.

'Why did he go there?' Giovanino asked.

His uncle raised his hand to his mouth, as though he were putting something into it, and shook his head. 'Why do you think? To feed his family of course. He went there for one year and laboured for three plastermen. When he came back, he brought a gramophone with him.' He smiled and made a winding motion with his hand. It was the second time Giovanino had ever seen him smile. The first time was when he won some money in the village lottery and bought the young mule. 'You turn a handle,' he said. 'Then place a disk on top and music comes from it; it passes into a needle and out through a shiny brass horn!' Zio Nicole hopped from one foot to another and began to sing and dance. 'Turintuli turintula.'

'And what does he do now?'

Zio Nicole stopped dancing and his smile vanished. 'He bought a piece of land, down there,' and pointed to the valley. 'Now he goes with his mule like everyone else and digs all day.'

Giovanino looked down at the road winding itself back and forth around the hairpins and saw, scattered along it, other mules and donkeys, led by men with bowed heads. Some had women and children walking alongside too. He turned and looked back the way he'd come and saw others following behind. Matilda shook her head and gave out a tired eeaaw. A deep murmuring sound began to follow them from behind, growing louder. Giovanino recognized the sound of Tonino's taxi straight away. It was the only vehicle in the village. Zio Nicole pulled his mule to the side of the road. Giovanino did likewise with Matilda. The taxi drew level with them and slowed down. Zio Nicole looked up and touched his cap to the Mayor who was sitting in the back. Giovanino did the same. Tonino gave a toot on his horn and they passed. They continued to walk side by side, silently watching the taxi, as it drove slowly past each family in turn. The people made room for the taxi to pass and showed their respect. It speeded up between each hairpin bend. Gradually it grew smaller and smaller until eventually it reached the valley below and vanished into the dust it threw up.

'Where are they going?' Giovanino asked.

'To Matera.'

'What do they do there?'

'All the mayors and officials from the villages roundabout meet there,' he said and gestured with his hand to the patches of white that broke up the ochre-coloured mountains. 'Salandria, Accettura, Calciano, Grottolle… They all send someone to discuss their taxes.'

'Taxes? What are taxes?' Giovanino asked.

'Huh! Taxes. You don't know what taxes are?' Zio Nicole shook his head and spat onto the ground bitterly. 'Each year collectors visit the villages and take money. If you have no money, they take a goat, a hen, a rabbit, a bottle of olive oil… Anything they can get their hands on.'

'Does my father pay taxes?' Giovanino asked.

'Yes, your father pays taxes. Everyone pays taxes.'

Zio Nicole walked in front silently. Giovanino followed, mesmerized by the rise and fall of the mule's hooves and the sweep of its tail. He was imagining tax collectors; men with furtive faces like foxes, prowling the villages at night, then leaving before anyone woke up, with chickens and rabbits under their arms and bottles of olive oil sticking out of their coat pockets, leading goats down the mountain roads.

'Zio Nicole, where do all the taxes go?' he shouted.

'They're shared out between the mayors and the officials and all the sirs and madams in Rome.' Zio Nicole shouted back without turning his head. 'Now save your energy for walking or you'll have none left for working.'

Giovanino looked around him. The hairpins they had turned, had brought the village back into view, now much smaller in the distance above his head. The forest canopy in the valley below was becoming larger. He caught up with Zio Nicole and walked alongside him limping.

Zio Nicole shook his head and sighed, then pulled his mule to one side.

'It's my big toe,' Giovanino said, pulling off his shoe and sock. Zio Nicole took a rag from his pocket that he used as a handkerchief, tore off a strip and folded it into a wad. Giovanino quickly dabbed at the blood on the knuckle, then laid the wad on top and replaced his sock and shoe.

'How much longer will it take me to reach the forest?' Giovanino asked, still limping beside him.

'You're about a quarter of the way there.' His uncle replied without looking round or changing his pace.

'Tomorrow at school,' Giovanino said. 'Professor Lombardi is going to teach me algebra.'

His uncle shook his head and increased his pace without replying.

'If I work hard today and fetch a good load of firewood I'll be able to go to school tomorrow and do mathematics.' Giovanino changed the way he placed his foot on the ground, lowering the outside first to avoid pressure. Because he wondered if Zio Nicole was angry at having to stop, he walked along silently for a while, thinking about what Professor Lombardi had told him about Albert Einstein – but then he couldn't keep quiet any longer.

'Zio Nicole, did you know that light is bent by gravity?' He shouted the words, unable to stop himself. 'A man called Albert Einstein has proved it. And did you know that gravity is a force that moves two bodies together?

Zio Nicole shook his head and looked up at the sky uncomprehendingly.

'Astronomers went to South America to photograph stars during a total eclipse,' Giovanino said. 'When they developed the plates into photographs they found the stars were somewhere different!'

Zio Nicole looked at him, then looked back down at the road without slowing his pace. Giovanino continued to limp alongside him.

'A total eclipse is when the moon passes between the earth and the sun,' Giovanino said, raising his hands. He pulled at Matilda's lead rein without realising it. She lifted her head and shook it. 'It only happens once every so many years and you can only see it in certain countries. Albert Einstein has worked out the speed of light.' He pulled at Zio Nicole's sleeve. 'He says that if you travel faster than the speed of light time goes backwards and you become younger!'

Zio Nicole stopped. His eyes had a strange look. He raised his hand. Giovanino stood there bewildered. A few seconds past before he realized that his uncle had slapped his face. Then his smile crumpled.

'Albert Einstein won't put food in your belly,' Zio Nicole shouted. 'The sun, the moon,' he looked up at the sky, then back down to Giovanino. 'You can talk about them as much as you like, will they gather your firewood? Will the sun and moon put food in your belly? Now stop this talk of mathematics. You weren't born for mathematics. You were born to dig, like your father and me and everyone else around here. What good is mathematics to us? Huh. Answer me that.' He shrugged his shoulders and held out his empty

blistered palms. 'Mathematics is for the sirs and madams in Rome.'
He turned sharply, then pulled at his mule's rein and strutted off.
Giovanino stood still, watching, then followed behind, limping.

The valley floor trapped the sun and became like an oven. In the
distance, where the track split into two, a stone bridge spanned a
dried-up riverbed. An olive tree stood to one side; its pale green
leaves shimmered in the heat haze like flames. The other peasants
travelling the road ahead of them had dispersed in different
directions and dotted the valley like clusters of insects. Giovanino
had heard of the flaming olive tree from stories, but had never seen
it, apart from in his imagination. He held it in his sight and
continued to limp at some distance behind Zio Nicole. Zio Nicole
paused, removed his cap and used it to wipe the sweat from his
face. He stared at the flaming olive tree also, then looked back at
Giovanino. Giovanino continued for a while, then stopped a safe
distance away. Zio Nicole's face had softened a little and he
beckoned for him to come closer. Giovanino limped the few
remaining paces until they were standing opposite each other. The
tears had dried on his cheeks and left white streaks either side of
his brown face.

Zio Nicole stooped down before him so that their faces were
level and held out his open palms; he touched his thumb and finger
tips together and shook them up and down slowly as though the
gesture reflected the meagreness of the terrain around them.

'Listen Giovanino,' he said. 'Do you think that you are the first
person to have shed those tears?' Giovanino shook his head. 'No,
your father and me, we have both shed those same tears many
times. It has been the same for our brothers and grandfathers and
all the men in these parts. Who knows for how many centuries
things have been this way? There is only one life for the men
here… We go out each day and labour. We throw our sweat and
blood onto the earth. And when the women and girls are done with

their cooking and sewing, they come too. There is only one way to escape… You have to harden your heart and forget about your family - then take one of those ships and emigrate to America or Australia. You must never weaken and become homesick or long to see your mother and father, or your sisters, or some pretty girl. If you come back, you'll be worse off than before because by then you will have seen how civilized people live and this desolate land will break you to its will.'

Giovanino stared at his uncle, not knowing what to say. A silence hung over the valley. Then the flaming olive tree claimed his attention and he turned towards it.

His uncle looked up at the sky, noting the position of the sun and the time of day. 'Let's go,' he said. And they walked silently towards the tree. Its leaves shimmered even more brightly in the haze as though it were on fire. Giovanino stared mesmerized, unaware of the time passing or his painful foot as the tree grew larger and more radiant with each step he took until they reached the bridge. Zio Nicole went to cross first. He let go of the lead rein and held onto the mule's tail, then he let it pull him up the steep incline until they disappeared over the brow. Giovanino held Matilda's tail tightly with both hands and crossed also. When he looked up again, the olive tree stood dull and ordinary before him.

'Huh,' said his uncle. 'So the flaming olive tree has fooled you too? It blazes from a distance like Moses' burning bush, as though God were going to talk to you from it. Then when you arrive it looks just like any other olive tree.'

Giovanino went closer and saw framed pictures of saints laid all around its trunk and coloured ribbons, torn and shredded by the weather, tied to its branches. 'Is this a religious tree?' he asked.

Zio Nicole shrugged. 'Father Pasquale says so but who knows? It's best not to take any chances,' He crossed himself.

Giovanino did the same.

His uncle pointed straight ahead, to where the track led towards the forest. Its green canopy was beginning to loom larger in the ochre valley and seemed to Giovanino like a magic city.

'There,' Zio Nicole said, pointing. 'You know what to do. When you've loaded the ass you can go home.' He turned the way they'd come and looked back up to the village, which was a patch of white, tiny and indistinct on top of the bare hill. 'You can't lose yourself. Just follow the track until you reach the foot of the mountain and keep climbing. If you get tired hold onto Matilda's tail and let her do the work.' He pulled at his mule's rein and went off where the track forked towards his land. Giovanino watched them for a while growing slowly smaller and smaller in the distance. Then he limped with Matilda to the forest.

Dull light filtered through the leaves and made shadows on the forest floor. The sweat started to turn cold on Giovanino's body and made him shiver. He stopped at a cypress that had snapped its trunk during a storm and leaned against it, inhaling its resinous scent. A horsefly tried to settle on Matilda's rump. She flicked her tail and threw her head backwards past the saddle, reaching at the fly with her tongue. A green pinecone the size of a fist lay in the leaf litter, partly buried. Giovanino noticed it at once and picked it up. He examined it, following the spiral patterns of seeds, which began with tiny seeds at its base, grew larger towards its middle, then became small again towards its crown. He imagined the spirals continuing endlessly as if by some predetermined formula, each seed's size and shape determined by the previous one. Then he looked at the snapped cypress trunk and saw the rings representing each year's growth and began to compare each seed in the spiral with the passing of time and wondered how long the forest had been there. Then he wondered how the village and the people living there came to be. Who had built the first house and where had they come from? 'I will take the cone to school tomorrow,' he thought, putting it into his pocket, 'and show it to

Professor Lombardi. He will understand the spirals and explain them with mathematics.'

He took his axe from Matilda's saddle and began hacking at the branches where they joined the trunk, then chopped them into logs the length of Matilda's body. When a pile had gathered, he took the bill-hook and began trimming the green needles from the twiggy ends of the branches that remained. The resin stuck to his fingers. He held his hands to his face and breathed in deeply, enjoying the smell, then wiped them on his baggy trousers. The sun was directly overhead. He unwrapped his bread and crushed tomato, leaned against the cypress trunk and ate. Then he wondered whether he should rest and travel back later in the cool, or load Matilda and walk home straightaway, so that he could take his slate and practice some mathematics before evening. He took the pine cone from his pocket and ran his finger over the seeds again, following the spirals. 'I'll draw the seeds exactly the size and shape they are,' he thought. 'Then, when I've drawn the biggest one, I will try to calculate the size of the next one.' He put the cone back into his pocket and began loading the heavier logs onto Matilda's back. When the pile was level with her neck, he tied it fast with a twine and began throwing the twiggy branches on top. The load was up past her head and, from behind, only her legs and tail were visible. He wedged his axe and bill-hook into the load and pulled at Matilda's rein. She refused to move.

He pulled again.

Again, she refused to move and hung her head low.

'Please Matilda,' he pleaded, pulling harder.

She continued to stand still. Reluctantly, he clenched his fist, as his father had shown him and held it to her muzzle.

She closed her eyes. He drew back his fist, then pulled sharply at her rein and they continued.

Giovanino raised his hand to shield his eyes from the glare, then looked back at the forest, which was still close enough for him to smell the leaves and pine needles. Then he looked up at the village, tiny and lost in the distance. He wondered whether to change his mind and return to the forest to rest a while in the shade until the day began to cool. He shifted his weight from one foot to the other to ease his painful toe, then took off his shoe and sock, unwound the bloodied cloth and examined the grazed knuckle joint. 'If I walk back to the forest, I'll waste the time and steps I have already taken,' he thought, 'and then I'll have to walk them over again. No, I'll walk as far as the bridge with the flaming olive tree.' he decided. 'Then, if the heat is too much, I'll rest beneath the olive tree, or beneath the bridge in the dried up river bed.' He wound the cloth back round his toe and limped off, staring at the ground. Matilda followed behind, nodding her head up and down.

Each time he raised his head to look up, the village continued to look tiny and indistinct. Giovanino decided to look out for the olive tree instead, wondering if it would seem on fire. He cupped his hand over his eyes and stared into the remoteness until eventually he saw a tiny orb glowing in the distance. At first, he thought it was his mind playing tricks on him. 'I'll keep my eyes on the ball of light,' he thought, 'and not take them off. Then perhaps the olive tree will continue to burn until I reach it. I won't even blink because the last time I took my eyes off it, just to cross the bridge, the flames vanished in a second.' He limped towards it, then, unable to prevent himself blinking, he decided to close first one eye and then the other, one at a time, in turn, so as not to lose sight of the tree for a moment. The flames grew slowly larger with the rhythm of his footsteps and the even rising and falling of Matilda's head, until he could make out the tree's trunk, brown and gnarled beneath the glowing canopy. He stopped, unable to move any closer because of the heat coming from it, mesmerised by the radiance, until he couldn't bear it any longer and turned for a moment towards the bridge. When he looked back, the tree had become as green and ordinary as any other olive tree, except for the ribbons tied to its branches and the pictures of saints lying around it on the ground. Giovanino wondered if he had imagined the flames and walked around the tree's trunk disappointed, examining it carefully. He pushed his fingers into the fissures of its bark and rubbed the leaves between his fingers. Then he looked up towards the village; the towers of its two churches, one at the high part and one below, now discernible above the sprawl of houses. He reached into his pocket and felt the pine cone, running his fingers over the seeds, imagining how he would draw it and decided to go on. He led Matilda to the bridge, then let her reins fall to the ground and followed behind, holding onto her tail, urging her forward with shouts.

'Eeeshaa, eeeshaa, Matilda,' he called. And Matilda began to climb the steep humpback until her ears and then her head became visible to him above her load. 'Eeeshaa,' he called again.

Matilda eeaawed in a way he had never heard before. Giovanino didn't realise that the steep angle of the bridge, and the force of him pulling at her load from behind, were causing her front hooves to leave the ground, until her hind legs crumpled and she reared up and fell backwards onto the ground, almost on top of him. The firewood lay beneath her like the shell of a great beetle and her legs flailed in the air above. Giovanino threw himself to one side. Matilda eeeaawed in helpless panic, until she was exhausted, then her head hung down; not even her ears touched the ground below her. Her stomach began to swell and the saddle strap cut into her. Giovanino pulled hard at the end, trying to unfasten the buckle, but the harder he pulled the more swollen her stomach became. She let out an exhausted eeeaaw, balls of dung rolled out of her, then her bladder opened and urine soaked the ground. He pushed futilely against her with his shoulder, then collapsed exhausted beside her, sobbing. The olive tree started to blaze once more and the sun shone more brightly, causing auras to arise, until he couldn't stand the radiance any longer. Then his epilepsy took him over and he bit his tongue. Some blood and saliva dribbled down his chin, he shook for a while, then lay on the ground unconscious beside the ass.

A knot of flies appeared from nowhere, attracted by the dung and began attaching themselves to the soft flesh of Matilda's vulva and anus, burrowing into her with their barbed proboscises. The sun passed slowly overhead, witnessing their work. Matilda whined, her tongue hung out of her mouth and her legs bent at the joints like broken branches.

Mathematics
(part two)

Zio Nicole stood with his back to the sun and pressed his hands down hard on the iron handles of his plough. The harness stretched taut against his mule's chest. Its hooves dug into the dry earth. The beast strained and a roll of earth rose up against the shiny metal ploughshare and fell in a long furrow. He continued to the end of the furrow, then called to his mule and turned. On one side, his field lay turned in rows of ochre furrows, on the other there was yellow corn stubble, scythed close to the ground with a few sparse wild flowers in between, tiny, and bright scarlet. The tip of the ploughshare cut into the earth again. He pressed down with his hands, forcing the plough deeper into the ground. With one eye he watched the yellow corn stubble fold over beneath him, while the other eye squinted into the sun, judging the straightness of his work. Half-way along the furrow a fatigue started to come over him. His hands slowly lost their power to grip and his legs began to tremble. The leather traces became slack, then fell either side of the mule. The beast ceased its straining. Zio Nicole dried the sweat on his face with his sleeve, then trampled down a patch of spikey corn stubble with his boot and sat down with his feet in the bare earth. He closed his eyes and rested his head in his hands. The calling of the cicadas, high-pitched and relentless, filled the air and began to aggravate him. Then, sensing that he was not alone, he looked up. A woman stood a few paces from him with her back to the sun, casting her shadow over him. Zio Nicole judged her to be about forty years old. She was not bent over like older women back at the village. Neither was she dressed in black. Instead she wore a long, blue dress. Her hair was still dark, wound into a knot on her head, and her feet were bare.

'Where have you come from?' he asked.

The woman looked around her and gestured with her hand, in a sweep that took in the whole valley and all the mountains. 'From there,' she replied.

Zio Nicole looked around in all directions. There were no other people to be seen and no kind of transport. He looked at her bare feet that were not cut or worn and realized that she could not have walked there. Neither was she perspiring or tired. Instead, she looked calm and serene. Zio Nicole didn't know why but he suddenly suspected that she could read his thoughts. He judged her to be beautiful. The woman smiled and he began to blush. Then she stepped forward and touched his shoulder gently with her hand and said, 'I think it's time to return to the village.' She smiled again, then turned and began to walk away.

Zio Nicole wanted to ask why but remained silent, awed by her calmness. He watched her strolling into the distance until it seemed to him that her feet no longer touched the ground. The calling of the cicadas grew louder and more intense. His heart began to beat so hard that he could hear it. Then his hands began to tremble. A great wave welled up inside him, then broke. The cicadas suddenly stopped their calling and the valley became silent. He looked all around him. The woman had vanished. He wondered if he had really seen her and began to feel foolish. The mule bowed, then raised its head, causing the bridle chain to jingle, attracting his attention. He quickly pulled a rag from his pocket and blew his nose. Then he set to work unfastening the buckles until the traces and then the harness fell to the ground. He was certain of one thing, that he must return straightaway. He led the mule forward, then threw himself onto its back and rode off, leaving the plough just as

71

it was, wedged in the ground, the ochre furrows on one side and the yellow corn stubble on the other.

Zio Nicole leaned over his nephew's sun-burnt face and slapped him. Giovanino opened his eyes slowly. They rolled in their sockets and he sank back into a stupor. Zio Nicole slapped him again. Then, seeing that he would not wake, he pinched his ear with his thumb-nail. A bead of blood appeared on Giovanino's ear lobe. The boy slapped at it with his hand as though he had been stung by a wasp and began to cry. Zio Nicole sat him up, then laid his hand on Matilda's upturned stomach and pulled hard at her saddle-strap. The buckle dug into her. He drove his knee into her belly. She winced. He drove it in again, harder this time, making her inhale sharply and the pin slipped free. He leant against her and pushed with his shoulder until she rolled silently off the pile of firewood and lay prostrate beside it. Zio Nicole screwed up his nose. There was an odour, putrid and disgusting; he followed it to her rear end, then saw the flies attached to her like a gall and retched. He began swiping at them with his cap. Some flies flew off but most of them remained. He pulled them off with his fingers and crushed them in his hands, then spat into his palms, intending to wash them off, but only succeeded in creating a slime. He retched again, then twisted Matilda's tail sharply. Her head lay in the dirt. He gave her tail another twist.

'For the love of God!' he shouted, and ran around to her head and twisted her ears in turn, then both at the same time. She didn't move or make a sound. He blew into one of her nostrils. Snot flew out of the opposite one and covered his cheek. He wiped it off, then put up a hand to protect his face and blew again into the other one. More snot blew out. He wiped his hand on the ground and continued to blow, in short, sharp bursts. Matilda started to snort as though an insect had crawled into her nostrils. Zio Nicole took her head, raised it up, then blew into both her nostrils in turn, slapping her face at the same time. She snorted once more, angrily this time, then shook herself.

'Come on Matilda!' he shouted and continued slapping her face in a gentle and encouraging way. Then he pushed his shoulder into her chest and forced her up. She unfolded her front legs, trembled uncertainly and began raising herself.

'Quickly Giovanino, come here,' he called.

Giovanino stumbled over. He held Matilda's head and began stroking her. 'Please Matilda,' he pleaded. 'Please, please stand up.'

Zio Nicole went back round to Matilda's rear-end and forced his shoulder under her until she was standing on all fours. He supported her for a while then let her stand. She trembled uncertainly and shook her head. Then she eeaawed forlornly and began to swish her tail at the flies that were trying to settle on her again.

Giovanino cried out: 'Bravo Matilda!' Then wrapped his arms around her neck.

Zio Nicole turned sharply from behind the ass, then raised his hand which was still covered with blood and crushed flies. 'How did Matilda come to be on her back?' he bellowed. His voice filled the valley for a moment then died away.

Giovanino flinched back, bewildered, and put up his arm to protect himself.

Zio Nicole suddenly recalled the woman he had seen earlier. He remembered how she read his thoughts, then how she told him to return to the village. He realised that, without her, Giovanino and Matilda would have been lying there until evening. His temper calmed. He stooped down so that his face was close to Giovanino's. The olive tree stood behind them with the mountains and the blue sky behind. Zio Nicole turned towards it.

'Who knows,' he said. He took off his cap and scratched his head thoughtfully. Then he crossed himself. Giovanino did the same.

The mule shuffled from side to side and flicked its hooves, then eeaawed objectionably. Zio Nicole pulled roughly at its harness. 'Keep still unless you want to end up as meat on our plates,' he shouted. 'Giovanino, hold this bridle.'

Giovanino stumbled towards him, still dazed from the fit, and steadied the animal's head. Zio Nicole flung Matilda's saddle onto the mule's back and began loading the firewood onto it, he tied it tightly with a twine, then tied Matilda's lead rein to the mule's tail.

'Come on Giovanino,' he called and they set off in a caravan, with Giovanino limping alongside. Zio Nicole looked around at the mountains and at the village in the distance perched on top of one of them, then he looked down at Giovanino. 'What is it?' he asked. 'Still the toe?'

Giovanino nodded, then sat on the ground. He removed his shoe and sock and unwound the bloodied cloth from around his toe.

'Does it hurt?' His uncle asked.

Giovanino shrugged his shoulders at first, then looked up and nodded his head.

Zio Nicole tore another strip from the cloth he used as a handkerchief, spat on it and wiped the bloodied knuckle joint. He pursed his lips and inhaled sharply, then smiled and shook his head. 'Do you think you'll make it?'

Giovanino shrugged his shoulders again.

Zio Nicole took off his cap, wiped the sweat from his forehead with it and put it back on. Then he folded the strip of cloth into a thick wad and laid it over the toe. Giovanino replaced his shoe and sock and stumbled alongside. His uncle took his hand. They walked a little more, then he stopped and crouched down. He touched his shoulder and Giovanino climbed onto his back. Zio Nicole stood up. He wound the mule's lead rein tightly around his wrist, then clasped his hands tightly behind him and carried his nephew piggy back, with the beasts following behind. The sweat on his back soaked his shirt. Giovanino fell asleep with his head resting against his uncle's neck. He was sweating too. Their sweat soaked through both their shirts and became mixed together.

Zio Nicole began to think about the woman again, wondering if she was real. Then he began to doubt that he had really seen her. 'Does it matter if she was real or not?' he thought, 'Without her, the boy and the donkey could have died in the sun.' Then he remembered how she had read his thoughts. 'She must have been a Saint,' he said to himself. 'As soon as I get back to the village, I'll go to Father Pasquale's house. I'll tell him everything, how the woman appeared from nowhere, that she was beautiful and that her feet were bare. I'll tell him she read my thoughts and how, when she walked off, her feet left the ground. Yes, I'll tell him that I've seen a Saint!' He trudged on. His thoughts calmed, then he remembered Netto, the cobbler's son. *He'd* seen the Madonna more than once, always at the same place, where the road forked towards the cemetery. Netto had gone lots of times to speak with Father Pasquale and now he was in an asylum… Zio Nicole began to feel fearful. Giovanino slipped down his back. Zio Nicole pushed him back up and rearranged his grip. 'I must be careful what I tell Father Pasquale,' he thought. 'I won't go to his house. No, I'll wait until I meet him in the street. I'll let him talk, then perhaps I'll say something and Father Pasquale will himself mention a Saint; he often does, St Rocco or St Antonio. Then I'll say I've heard that some people have seen Saints, even here in this part of Italy. How would someone know if they've really seen a Saint? He won't suspect a thing. I'll let him talk, perhaps he'll say that Saints can read your thoughts, then I'll know. Or I'll say I've heard that Jesus walked on water. He will say, "Yes, that's true."

And I will ask if Saints can walk on water also? If he says "Yes," or scratches his head, the way he does when he is thinking deeply and says, "Yes, maybe." I will ask if Jesus could walk along without his feet touching the ground. I'm sure he will say, "Yes, Jesus could do whatever he wanted to do." Then I will ask if he thinks Saints can walk without their feet touching the ground also. If he says they can, then I'll know.' Zio Nicole started to feel uneasy again and thought, 'No, I don't want Father Pasquale to suspect anything. I won't ask him so many questions. That will be best. I'll just let him talk and, if I don't find out what I want straightaway, then I'll bide my time and ask just a little bit more every time we meet. Not too much though, that way he won't suspect anything.'

His shoulders and neck started to ache. He looked up at the village with its white-washed houses. All their features, the window shutters and the doors, were becoming distinct. Soon he would be at the foot of the mountain and would begin climbing the hairpins. He crouched down, carefully so as not to wake Giovanino, and let his feet touch the ground to relieve the weight. He pictured the woman in his mind. 'She was so serene,' he thought and imagined her to be kind. 'There's no kindness in the village, not like that.' He looked around him at the mountains and at the villages perched on top of them, wondering if it was different anywhere else. Then he shook his head. 'No,' he thought, 'how could it be any different?' and picked up his nephew again, in his arms this time, and continued on his way.

Giovanino's face rested against his cheek. The boy's hot breath reminded him of his wife, Appollonia, when they lay together in bed. The mule, then the ass, followed behind with their heads bowed. Zio Nicole wondered whether to tell his wife about the woman. 'No, she'll worry,' he thought. Then he realised that he felt happy despite his misfortunes. That his heart felt not just full, but bursting. The way it did when he first fell in love with Apollonia, only much more so. Meeting the woman had made him feel like this. Tears filled his eyes. He quickly wiped them away with the back of his hand, relieved that Giovanino wasn't awake to see. Then he felt something hard digging into his chest. Zio Nicole pushed his hand inside Giovanino's pocket and pulled out the pine cone. He looked at it for a moment, judged it to be useless, and let it fall to the ground.

The mule protested at the weight of its load and the steep incline of the hairpins; it threw its head from side to side and eeaawed. Zio Nicole pulled down roughly with the rein, then took a cypress twig from its back and beat its rump. The beast eeaawed again, languidly this time, and continued obediently. Giovanino slipped repeatedly from his grasp; he forced him back up, rearranging his grip every time, sometimes his fingers were interlocked, other times his palms grasped one another. Each rearrangement of the boy's body brought relief to one part of his body and pain to another. He laid Giovanino's head on his right shoulder for a while, then on the left, until he could continue no longer and had to lower him to the ground. He looked up at the sun and stretched himself. There would be no shade until they reached the village. He took his water jug from the mule's saddle and shook it. Only a little water splashed in the bottom. He shook his nephew gently to wake him, then passed him the jug. Giovanino threw his head back without speaking and drank thoughtlessly until the jug was empty, then handed it back to his uncle.

'Oh well,' Zio Nicole muttered and ran his tongue over his parched lips. He studied the ass, wondering if he could sit the boy on its back, but her head was bowed more than was normal and her legs still trembled.

'I can walk now,' said Giovanino. He stood up, took a few steps and stumbled onto his hands and knees.

'Take it easy, Giovanino.' His uncle stretched his long back, then pulled at his shirt to let some air circulate between his body and the coarse fabric. He crouched down again and Giovanino climbed onto his back. Zio Nicole looked up at the village; in a while he would enter its streets and smell the wood-smoke and the goats and pigs that wandered there. He looked back the way he'd come, at the winding hairpins, then at the valley below, to the forest, barely distinct now, and to where he sensed his abandoned plough to be. Then he thought of the woman again and the flaming olive tree. He turned and resumed his trudging. 'I won't stop until I reach the village,' he thought. 'And when I arrive, I'll take the road to the back of Giovanino's house and unload the wood there before I take him home. That way his father won't see Matilda returning unloaded. It's best that he never knows about the mishap on the bridge, otherwise Giovanino will be sure of a beating. And later on, after I've eaten, when Apollonia is out of the house visiting her mother and father, I'll close the door and take her wedding dress out of the chest and cut a tiny piece of white ribbon from it, from the hem where she won't notice and tomorrow when I return to my ploughing and pass the olive tree, I'll tie it to a branch.'

Giovanino's head lay on his uncle's shoulder. He slipped down a little. Zio Nicole pushed him back up and gripped his hands even more tightly beneath him. The track in front of him rose and fell before his eyes with the rhythm of his walking. He began repeating the words, 'Beautiful, barefoot woman - ' silently to himself with the rhythm of his footsteps, over and over as if it were a prayer.

Zio Nicole unloaded the last log from his mule's back and added it to the pile at the back of Giovanino's house. He stretched himself, then sat down on top of the log-pile. The mule bowed its head, relieved, and for a moment, it sounded as though a few notes of music fell from its bridle chain. Matilda stood behind, with her lead-rein still tied to its tail, enjoying the shade. Giovanino stroked her face and petted her ears.

'Better that your father never knows about your mishap with Matilda,' said Zio Nicole. 'Otherwise he may well have a little present for you.'

Giovanino thought of the trousers and the cap his father gave in the morning and looked at his uncle confused. 'A little present?' he repeated.

'Yes, a little present.' His uncle showed him the palm of his hand, then shook his head.

Giovanino frowned.

Zio Nicole rested some more; then when he was ready, he stood up, took Giovanino's hand and walked with him to the front of the house. Giovanino limped over the threshold first and dragged a chair noisily over the floor and sat at the table, next to where his mother had laid a damp cloth over some dough. He folded his arms, then rested his head on them and immediately fell asleep. The commotion woke his father; he stretched and contorted his body without rising from his chair and saw his son. Then he looked up at Zio Nicole and tapped the side of his head and shrugged.

Zio Nicole nodded.

'Fucking epilepsy,' his father muttered.

'It happened on the way back. It's a good thing I found him, otherwise who knows.'

'What fucking luck.'

Zio Nicole shrugged. 'Yes, and the flies have been troubling the ass, all around her rear-end.' He said it casually as though it were something minor. 'I'll come back later with some tar and dab it on her.'

Filomena began to stir in her cradle; she cried gently, then settled again and the atmosphere softened. Her mother woke and began untangling herself from Rosina and Graziela's sleeping bodies up in the loft. She drew back the tattered curtain and saw Giovanino slumped over the table.

Her husband looked up at her and shook his head. 'Fucking curse,' he said.

She climbed down the ladder without replying, poured water from a jug and woke her son gently. He kissed her, drank slowly, then immediately laid his head back down and went to sleep. She leaned over him and kissed the top of his head, then removed the cloth from the table. Coils of floury dough covered the surface next to Giovanino's face. She cut them into pieces the thickness of her thumb, pressed her index finger into them and rolled them towards her, then quickly flicked them off, transformed into ear-shaped pieces of pasta. Her hair fell forward onto her face; she pushed it back, hardly stopping her work. Some flour dusted her cheek as the pile of pasta grew larger.

'Nicole, what are you doing tomorrow?' Giovanino's father asked.

'Tomorrow I have to finish my ploughing.'

'Giovanino needs to learn to plough. What do you think, Woman, will he be well enough to go with his uncle tomorrow?'

She looked up at the wooden crucifix hanging on the wall opposite and laid her free hand on Giovanino's shoulder. 'Perhaps,' she replied. 'If it's God's will.' She stopped her work, just long enough to cross herself, and touched her lips with her floury fingertips.

The Roman

The man on the radio just said this is the hottest day in Rome for twenty years. It's so stifling I could hardly breathe on my way back from school. The streets are deserted; everyone is staying indoors. The sheets on my bed are damp with sweat. Even with the door and window open there is no fresh air in my room. Looking across the hallway, into the kitchen, I can see my mother sitting at the table. There's a letter in front of her, next to a quickly torn-open envelope. She's smoking. Not the way she usually smokes, with long deep inhalations. Today she sits staring at the floor. The cigarette is burning down to a long finger of ash in her hand. I guess the letter is from my grandmother. I know that my grandfather is ill. He hasn't been able to think straight for months and now his lungs are bad too. I don't want my mother to know I've been watching her, so I walk in as usual.

I say; 'Ciao.'

She looks up. The ash falls from her cigarette without her noticing and makes a grey patch on the tiles. She stubs out her cigarette in the ash-tray, glances at the letter without speaking, then stands up and hugs me. Her perfume is mixed with the faint odour of her perspiration. Stepping back, she takes a deep breath, walks to the phone and calls my father. He works in Milan as a highway engineer. He goes wherever there's work. That's how he met my mother, building the bypass outside Matera, near her village. It's still difficult in the South for a woman to marry the man she wants, so we hardly ever visit my grandparents. When we do, my father never comes.

My mother speaks. 'This is Marietta Abbatelli. I want to talk to my husband.' Then after a pause. 'It's urgent.' She strokes her free hand down the side of her dress. He comes to the phone and she explains.

She says, 'I want to go tonight. Paolo can come with me. Gina needs to study, so she can stay the night with Laura.' There is another pause, then the usual 'I love you' and they hang up. She picks up her handbag, takes out her address book and a packet of cigarettes. Then she calls the station. A couple of minutes pass. There's no reply. She lights another cigarette before the station responds. She books our tickets for eleven fifteen, then sits back at the table and stares at the floor. My father is never around when we need him; he only comes home one weekend a month. Says it's because we need the money, otherwise we wouldn't be able to live like we do. He should be going with her, not me. I return to my room, lie down on my bed and continue watching her through the open door. It's getting hotter. Her dress is sticking to the sweat on her back.

My mother is flitting around the kitchen like a bird. I realise I've been asleep. My mouth tastes dirty. I walk into the kitchen. She embraces me, smelling clean and freshly showered. Then steps back, wrinkles her nose, goes to the cupboard and hands me a towel. I go to the bathroom. She holds up her finger, mimics brushing her teeth.

I come back into the kitchen. She is preparing salad. A pan of water and some sauce simmer on the stove; slices of meat make whispering noises under the grill. The water boils. She tips in some pasta and stirs the sauce at the same time. My mother keeps house like someone spinning plates. I set three places at the table. My sister walks in; she is always punctual. My mother explains everything.

'I'm going home tonight with Paolo. I want you to stay the night at Laura's.'

My sister smiles without meaning to. We are not close to our grandparents and this means she can spend time alone here with Marcello. He is a student from Florence. She looks away guiltily and begins to cry. My mother hugs her.

'It's Ok,' she says. 'I was young once.'

I feel uneasy with my sister. A couple of days ago I borrowed her Beatles album, their latest, Abbey Road, without her permission and damaged a couple of tracks. She hasn't noticed yet and this isn't the time to own up.

We eat quietly. Afterwards I wash up with my sister. My mother sits staring at the floor for a while then jumps up, lights a cigarette and goes to the dresser. She takes objects from the shelves, files them neatly into her handbag: some keys, her address book, hairbrush, make-up. Then, from deep in one of the drawers, pulls out a little silver pot. She unscrews the lid and tips out a roll of fifty thousand-lira notes into her hand, counts them, then buries them deep in her handbag. My sister packs a small overnight bag; her schoolbooks stick out the top. Laura lives in an apartment upstairs; they are both planning to go to university. There is a commotion of hugs and tears. My sister leaves, still looking a little guilty.

My mother goes to her room, returns with a suitcase and a pile of clothes draped over her arm. We go to my room. I take some clothes out of my wardrobe. She packs. Our underwear becomes mixed up together.

It's eight thirty. Our taxi is booked for ten. I watch T.V. My mother can't relax; she busies herself with housework. The doorbell rings. She answers it, exhausted. Every floor has been swept, the furniture polished, each ornament dusted and put back. The taxi driver eyes up my mother. She looks young for her age; sometimes people mistake her for my sister. My father hates it when men look at her. The look on her face tells him to fuck off. He sees me walk into the hall lugging the case and looks away shamefaced. We go into the street. He offers to carry the case. I refuse. The streets are busy now. I notice him glance at us a couple of times in his rear-view mirror. My mother stares out through the window. At the station he opens the door for her, calls her Signora, takes the case without asking and places it on a luggage trolley. She pays him. He thanks her in a polite, friendly way. They have made their peace.

The station is crowded. We queue for our tickets. A group of young soldiers stare at my mother. She avoids eye-contact, taps her hands on the bar of the luggage trolley. We collect our tickets and force our way through the crowds. The train is full. More soldiers stand in the corridor astride their packs. They move aside for us. We find a compartment occupied by middle-aged couples. There are two empty seats. I struggle to lift the case onto the luggage rack. A man gets up to help. I feel embarrassed. My mother sits opposite me, her face glowing with perspiration. She closes her eyes. Guards walk past outside, slamming the doors. There's some shouting, then a silence. A whistle - and the train rolls forward. It freewheels for a while, then heaves and freewheels again. The motion is comforting. The other passengers begin to relax. My mother falls asleep. The soldiers make me feel uneasy.

I think about our home. We live on the Via Nuova. The buildings there are at least two hundred years old! I think the name should be changed to the Via Vechia. My father says it's because it was new once; that everything starts off that way.The doors and window-shutters are painted dull blue, cracked and peeling like old leaves. My mother hates it, she wants to live somewhere modern.

My father says, 'But Marietta, when it rains the street looks like an oil painting.'

She gets annoyed, throws her hands in the air and replies, 'Oh yes, like an oil painting by Leonardo da Vinci.'

He is quiet for a while, says, 'Marietta, when you shout like that people can hear you all the way down to Naples.' She blushes, embarrassed. He says: 'All Southern women shout. They're made that way. They just can't help it.'

The train judders. Everyone is asleep. Through the window I can see the carriages trailing behind us, a long rope of glowing segments. Without realising it, my mother leans her head on the shoulder of the man next to her. Her mouth falls open, making her look ridiculous. We enter a station. The carriages heave noisily; brakes screech, everyone wakes up. The soldiers in the corridor stand up, rearrange their crumpled packs, and stretch. My mother walks past them to the lavatory. They let her pass, exchanging sleepy glances with one another. The train heaves forward, loses power, heaves again, slowly gains momentum. The soldiers sit back down on their packs. My mother returns, stepping over their feet. They look up at her. She walks past, stern-faced. I go next. Their smell reminds me of cooked onions. The lavatory is tiny, with barely enough room to stand. The train rocks, making me lose my balance and I piss on the floor. I'm not the only one. The floor is covered with urine. It's unpleasant to breathe. I press the flush, comb my hair; it's nearly down to my shoulders. I go back into the corridor. I have to step over the soldiers. They ignore me.

Back in the carriage, someone has opened the window. Cool air enters and night smells: hot metal and pine trees. The man sitting next to my mother offers to change seats with me. I nod, then sit beside my mother. She leans her head on my shoulder and holds my hand. The lady opposite smiles.

It's getting light. My mother is stretched out on the seats opposite, sleeping. The other passengers must have got off when I was asleep. The soldiers have vanished from the corridor. The train heaves and clanks as though it is empty. There is no breeze, only the smell of metal heating up. Outside the landscape is sparse and rugged, like a desert. Far off in the mountains, tiny patches of white, villages I guess, reflect the sun. I imagine the brigands my grandfather told me about when I was very young. I wonder how anyone can bear to live in a place like this.

We pull into Foggia. My mother continues to sleep. A vendor brings his tray sleepily to our window. I shake my head. He walks off, disappointed. An old man stands on the platform holding the reins of a pack mule. It spooks, kicking out its back legs, eeawing. He punches it in the mouth and walks off. It follows him obediently. The commotion wakes my mother. She crosses her arms over her chest and hunches her shoulders, as though protecting herself from something.

I say: 'Are you Ok?'

She nods her head and fakes a smile. I don't see anyone get on the train. She gets up and walks to the lavatory. The train clanks and heaves itself back into a rhythm. We are back in the sparse countryside. My mother returns. She sits staring through the window, puts her hand to her mouth and gently bites her knuckle. She has brushed and tied back her hair; removed all her make-up and jewellery, apart from her wedding ring.

There is a smell like cold, damp paper when we get off the train at Grassano station. It must be the river I saw as we approached. No one else gets off the train. A fat old man is dozing in his taxi. We look his way. He wakes up as though he has some sixth sense, shuffles towards us out of breath and grabs the case from me without asking. We get in his taxi. There is no space between his paunch and the steering wheel. On the dash-board is a magnetic icon of the Madonna. The winding road up the mountain is badly pitted with holes and we weave all over the road to avoid them. Coming towards us is a man my father's age. He is leading a donkey with a woman riding on the back. Her head is covered with a blue shawl. They remind me of Mary and Joseph. We carry on. It is impossible to avoid the holes. The magnetic Madonna slips and becomes cock-eyed. The taxi driver adjusts it, looks at us in his rear-view mirror, then up at the sky. He looks as though he is going to cross himself but doesn't. Either side of us is a desert of white chalk. The village is a white strip at the top of a bare hill. It makes me think of Nazareth and all the stuff I learned in Sunday school. My mother is staring down at the floor, fiddling with her wedding ring, twisting it round and round her finger.

I ask: 'Why does Grandfather disapprove of my father?'

She whispers: 'Because all the old men down here disapprove of everything.'

The taxi driver's eyes dart up to the rear-view mirror, then back onto the road. He still hasn't asked us where we want to go!

We stop outside my grandparents' house! I remember the old stable door from years ago. The taxi driver gets out, walks to the other side of the car and, thinking that I can't see, spits discreetly onto the road. A little boy with huge black eyes, his hair shorn close to his head, stares at me shyly from the doorway opposite. My mother pays the driver. He lifts out our case and stares at me as though he were a sympathetic relative. My grandmother opens the door, kisses us and starts sobbing as if on cue. I sense someone staring at us from behind a curtain at the window opposite. My mother senses it too and hustles us inside.

It is difficult not to screw up my face at the smell. The room is like a dank cellar. The floor is made of worn, uneven bricks, the walls are whitewashed and bare, apart from a crucifix and a picture of the Holy Virgin. My grandfather is sitting at the end of a table. He turns his head towards us slowly, and stares. His hair and moustache are slate grey. Veins stand out on the back of his hands and temples, like dark blue conduits. My mother seems afraid to move any closer. I walk towards him. She follows. His sharp tobacco breath greets us. We lean forward and kiss him. I am embarrassed by the smell of his urine.

My mother says: 'How are you, Papa?'

He replies: 'Oh, I don't know. They tell me I've got... Oh I don't know... What is it I've got?' He is silent. His sentence hangs in mid-air unfinished, as though shrouded in mist and if he waits long enough it will pass, leaving a word clear enough for him to read. My mother laughs without meaning to, then stops and looks at me. There is a silence.

I drag the case into the next room. There are two single beds. I strip down to my shorts and lie down. My mother comes in, slips the straps of her dress over her shoulders and lets it fall down to the floor. She steps out of it and lies down on the other bed.

I say: 'Why did you laugh back there?'

She is silent for a while as though the answer is lost somewhere deep inside her. Then she moves onto my bed and says, 'Oh, because for years I thought Alzheimer was the name of a wise old German philosopher.'

I say: 'Well, what's so funny?'

She wraps her arms around me, explains all about Alzheimer and starts to cry. It is quiet outside, too hot for people to be in the street. There are hardly any cars; we only passed two on the way here; a couple of beaten-up old Fiats. I've never seen anything like them in Rome. My mother is asleep. I'm relieved. I don't know how to be with her when she's like this. We are both damp with perspiration and her breath smells faintly metallic.

My mother is drying her hair; she is wearing a plain, modest dress. She leans over and kisses me. She smells clean and fresh. I go to the bathroom. There is no bath or shower. I wash myself all over, in the stone sink, with a flannel.

We go to the kitchen together. My grandfather is exactly where we left him but he's fast asleep. He is sitting upright like one of those portraits you see in the art museums. In front of him is a half-eaten fish on a tin plate. The head and tail are perfectly intact, held together by the bare skeleton. Beside it on the table-top is a slice of bread, broken up, like a jig-saw with some pieces missing. There is no sign of any cutlery, only a tin mug with a cloth draped over it. My grandmother brings two plates for us, each with a fish and a slice of bread. My mother puts her fish onto her bread and picks at it with her fingers, like a peasant woman. She would never act that way in Rome! My grandfather snores loudly and unexpectedly. We look at each other and almost laugh but stop ourselves. My grandmother makes a little church with her hands, looks at us, then at him, then up at the ceiling as though praying and shakes her head. I lick my fingers; they taste of salt and olive oil.

My grandfather wakes up, looks at us, then coughs and hawks noisily from the back of his throat. My grandmother uncovers the tin mug and passes it to him. He spits into it. She covers it again. I stare. My mother gives me a look. I look away. My grandfather struggles to his feet and looks directly at me.

'Paolo, you come with me,' he says.

My mother and grandmother exchange worried looks. I shrug my shoulders. Their expressions change and say, 'Well, what harm can it do?' He puts his hand on my shoulder and steers me to the door. It's so hot we cross the road so as to walk in the shade. We reach the end of the street. He leans against the building and coughs in a long high-pitched wheeze. A ball of gob dribbles out of his mouth onto the ground. I stare down at it. It is yellow, streaked with blood, like banana-ripple gelati. My stomach turns heavy and cold like ice. He looks at me sternly, scrapes dirt over it with his foot and gestures with his hand for me to move on. We get to the end of the next street. He stops again. His breathing is noisy and high-pitched. He coughs and spits again. This time I don't stare. The veins on his temple are throbbing. He recovers himself, leans his weight on my shoulder and steers me towards a barber shop.

We weave our way through the plastic streamers that hang in the doorway. It's cool inside and there is a pleasant smell of spirit and shaving soap. An old fan circulates the air; it makes a sound like a moth beating its wings against a windowpane. The barber has just finished shaving an old man. He's made him look brand new, despite his age and wrinkles. They look me up and down. The barber squeezes my shoulders and biceps.

'So who is this?' he says.

My grandfather replies: 'Marietta's boy.'

The barber looks me up and down some more, then asks: 'Who's his father?'

My grandfather shrugs his shoulders. 'The Roman.'

They all shake their heads!

'And what does he do?' asks the old man who looks brand new.

'He goes to school.'

They look at each other astonished!

The barber takes down a bottle of wine and four glasses from above his mirror. The glasses are greasy and badly stained. He pours. My grandfather makes a sign with his fingers. He half fills one and passes it to me. I want to please my grandfather, so drink with them. He smiles at me and gestures towards the barber's chair. The wine is making me confused. I sit in the chair so as not to offend him. The barber puts the cape over my shoulders.

I say, ' Ok. Just a centimeter off the ends.' My grandfather shakes his head. The barber puts the clippers next to my ear and runs them all over my head! My hair is falling onto the floor. He is shearing me like one of the village boys and I feel angry with my grandfather. I think of my father in Milan, working with his charts and levels; he should be here taking care of my mother. My face has turned red and mad-looking. I look at my grandfather's reflection in the mirror, sitting behind me. His breathing has become easier. He looks taller and is beaming with pride. The barber brushes me down.

'Is that all right for you?' he says.

I get up. Force myself to nod.

My grandfather pulls some screwed-up notes out of his pocket, peels one off and hands it to the barber. Then he stares at me and strokes his hand over my scalp affectionately.

'That's much better,' he says. 'I want to send you back to your father looking smart and tidy.'

We weave our way back through the plastic streamers. The street is like a furnace; beads of sweat form instantly on our faces. My grandfather stops every few meters and coughs up more of himself. Outside the house, he leans against the door, gathering himself. His breathing becomes more controlled; he nods. I lift the latch and enter. My mother is sitting at the table, reading. She looks up, sees my shorn scalp and stares in disbelief. A moment later she erupts, turning on my grandfather. I quickly raise my hand.

'It's Ok, Mother. I like it.'

Her temper subsides. I lead him to his room and he stumbles onto the bed. I help him roll over onto his back. My grandmother has followed us in, carrying the tin cup; a cloth is draped neatly over it to make it look respectable. She shoos me out of the room.

My mother stares at me, shaking her head. The sound of my grandfather coughing takes over the house. She covers her ears. I put my hands on her shoulders; hold her at arm's length. She smooths her hand over my head and I smile.

'It'll grow again soon,' I say.

It's evening. My grandfather has calmed down and the house is quiet. My grandmother is preparing supper. A pot of soup simmers on the stove; she cuts bread and arranges the doorsteps into a spiral on a tin plate. I sense she's glad that we've come but now she's ready for us to leave.

People are returning to the village with their mules. Their bridle-chains jingle like pockets of loose change, their eeawing is tired and frustrated and their hooves make clicking sounds on the cobbles. My mother drags our case in, then lays the table. The street is beginning to smell like a latrine. She closes the window while my grandfather stays in his room and we eat silently.

My grandmother clears the table. I hear the taxi bouncing over the cobbles. There is a short, almost polite, blast on the horn. My mother looks at me across the table then glances at the door of my grandfather's room. I go in to say goodbye. He is sitting propped up in bed, like an old king in a fairytale, staring into space. I walk over to him and realise he is crying. He takes my arm, pulls my face down to his, kisses me, then pushes me away. I walk back out. My mother searches anxiously through her handbag, pulls out a handkerchief, blows her nose and marches in. I look around the room, notice a series of lines drawn next to the door like high-tide markers. I read the name beside each one. The lowest one, less than a meter high, is my mother's, followed by a date; then all her brothers and sisters. They all emigrated years ago. I guess this is my grandmother's work. All the lines have been gone over again and again to stop them fading. My mother comes back in the room still holding the handkerchief. She pulls a face, for a moment she looks like a little girl and wipes her eyes.

My grandmother walks us outside. The taxi driver is leaning against his car, arms folded over his paunch.

My grandmother shakes her head and says, 'Best go back to Rome. This is no place for young people.'

There is a drama of hugs and tears. The taxi driver takes the case from me and puts it in the back. My mother gets in without acknowledging him. We bounce over the cobbles, in between rows of mules tethered to the houses on either side. People watch us from open doorways.

The train, all lit up, snakes its way towards the station below us. The driver, anticipating my mother's anxiety, looks into his rear-view mirror and says, 'Twenty minutes, Signora.'

She relaxes and holds my hand.

It's cooler by the station. The familiar smell of the river, like cold, wet newspaper, hangs in the air. A couple of guards, their trousers frayed and patched, stare at us. The taxi driver insists on carrying our case to the platform. My mother pays him and smiles for just a second and his pudgy face melts into a blush.

The carriages are mostly empty. I lug the case, following my mother along the corridor. A young woman with a little girl clutched under each arm like a mother-hen looks up at us. She and my mother make a pact with their eyes. We enter and sit down opposite. The girls look at me and bury their faces in their mother's dress. My mother introduces herself, then locks her fingers through mine and lifts up my hand as though I were a winning athlete.

'This is my son, Paolo,' she says.

The little girls crane their necks and peer at me nervously.

Foggia station is deserted and smells of yesterday's espressos and foccacias. The girls are sprawled either side of their mother, sleeping. She tells my mother how glad she is to be going home to Naples. The train rolls forward. They nod in agreement. The station passes by the window, getting faster. A look of relief replaces their tense expressions. My mother smiles at me for the first time since we left Rome.

'Try to get some sleep,' she says.

She gets up and goes to the lavatory. We are back in the countryside. There is fresh air coming in through the window and the smell of metal heating up. The woman looks at me, not knowing what to say, and smiles. My mother comes back into the compartment. Her hair is untied, resting on her shoulders; she has put back her make-up and jewellery. We notice the smell of her perfume. The woman comments on it. My mother hands her the bottle. She dabs a little on her wrists and behind her ears. The smell makes them smile. I feel as though I am preparing to hand my mother safely back to my father.

She is dozing, her head resting on my shoulder. Even sitting down, I notice that I'm about ten centimetres taller. Signs for Napoli station pass by the window. The woman places a hand on each of her sleeping daughters and shakes them gently. One of them starts to cry. The train goes quiet, loses power and begins to coast. The brakes make a long squeal and we stop. My mother wakes up, smiles at the crying girl and picks her up. They carry the sleepy bundles to the door. I follow with their luggage. A man, her husband I guess, greets them, relieved.

Back in the compartment a sleepy vendor lifts his tray up to our window.

My Mother asks, 'How much for two coffees and two foccacias?' Their smell makes me hungry.

He says, 'Two thousand lira.'

She turns away. People have boarded the train. There is a whistle, someone shouts, doors slam. The train moves slightly forward.

He shouts, 'Ok. Ok. Fifteen hundred.'

She takes the foccacias and coffees, hands them to me and holds up two one thousand lira notes. He goes to take them. She holds them out of reach. He gives her the change first. She pays him. He is walking to keep up.

Our compartment is full of sleeping passengers. The man opposite slouches into his seat as though he's melting. He wakes up, unfastens his belt and kicks off his shoes; his feet stink. My mother wakes up, wrinkles her nose and smiles at me like her old self.

It's light. We're all sprawled in our seats, our bodies overlapping. The sound of the train echoes against the buildings on either side. Rome is waking up; people are out on their balconies. The other passengers are waking up too; they look at each other awkwardly, straighten their clothes and comb their hair; the women take out little mirrors and put back their daytime faces.

Stationi Termini is teeming with people. I drag our case onto the platform. My mother follows, looking tired and relieved. We force our way through the crowds. Loudspeakers blast out announcements, a vendor pushes past with a tray-full of coffee cartons, froth spilling down their sides. My father calls out to us. She sees him and runs over. He holds out his arms and she melts into him. I catch her up with the case. My father stares at my shorn scalp and hugs me. Then he steps back and looks me up and down some more.

'Paolo, you've changed,' he says.

Fireworks

Pearl was sitting in front of a dressing-table, staring at her reflection. She and Vito were having some time together, travelling. It was Pearl's idea. 'It'd be best to do it, before the grandchildren come,' was how she'd put it. Mostly, she'd wanted to visit the village where Vito was born and maybe meet a relative or two. Vito had always made excuses. He even seemed secretly relieved when they couldn't afford to attend his mother's funeral. Pearl had never forgotten that. Then, after having been away for nearly fifty years, he finally caved in and agreed to go.

She applied her lipstick, then brushed her blonde hair and parted it, examining the roots. She'd had them done a couple of days before they left America. Satisfied they wouldn't need doing again until they reached Rome, she got up and twirled around. Her skirt clung tightly to her girdle.

'Do you think I look ok in this, Honey?' she asked.

Vito sighed while her back was turned.

'You look great,' he said, as she turned to face him.

Vito loaded their cases into the white Alfa Romeo convertible they'd hired. The hood was down and Pearl had tied back her hair. Vito shook hands with the two brothers who owned the pension where they'd been staying, and told them they'd be back in a couple of days.

A couple of hours later they approached the first hair-pin bend leading up to Vito's village. He tried to change down a gear. There was a crunching sound, the car slowed then lurched forward.

'It's a manual, Honey,' Pearl said.

Vito took a breath. 'I asked them for an automatic.'

'Would you like me to drive?'

'No thanks.'

Pearl pushed her sun-glasses up onto her head, to get a better look at the view. The village was painted white and there were two churches, one slightly taller than the other, with spires at either end. She turned her head, taking in the other villages perched on the mountain sides. The air was fresh, and she was smiling in anticipation of the good time she imagined lay ahead.

Vito slowed as they approached another hair-pin, then pulled over and stopped.

'What are you doing, Honey?' She turned and looked down over the edge for the first time, into the valley with its winding river-bed and railway line. There were some red-roofed buildings that formed a train station. A train was slowly pulling out.

'Why have we stopped?'

Before he could reply, an old man leading a donkey walked by the side of the car. The donkey was nodding its head in time with its foot-steps. There was an old woman sitting side-saddle on the donkey's back. She was wearing a long, black dress that came down to her leather work-boots and a black shawl that covered her head and shoulders. She stared at Pearl as she passed and Pearl stared back. They made eye-contact for a moment, then the moment passed. Pearl slumped back into her seat and pulled her sun-glasses back down over her eyes.

'I told you the place would still be pretty backward,' Vito said.

***

Gianni, a short, fat man, with bowed, matchstick legs, was bent over, placing fireworks into metal tubes that he'd dug into the ground the day before. He was breathing heavily and massaged his back every time he stood upright. Vito pinched out his cigarette and put it into his tin, alongside two others, and scrambled down the path. Gianni turned and looked at Vito, then he looked up at the village where Vito had come from. The sun was in Gianni's eyes and he was sweating. He took off his cap, wiped his face with it and put it back on his bald head.

'Do you need some help?' Vito asked.

Gianni looked along the rows of empty tubes, then at the bags of fireworks that still needed to be carried.

'The round ones are Starbursts and the square ones are Roman Candles,' he said indifferently, holding up the various fireworks for Vito to see, naming them. 'Do you think you'll be able to remember them?'

'Of course,' Vito replied.

Gianni kept his wallet in his back pocket. It was fat and bulging with notes. Vito carried the bags of fireworks and followed behind, handing him whatever fire-works he asked for, unable to ignore it.

When they were done, they both scrambled back up the path.

Vito looked up at Gianni expectantly.

Gianni slapped his pockets. Then he pulled out some coins, gave them to Vito and walked off towards the pension, where he was staying.

Vito stared at the coins, then he stared at the wallet, riding up and down in Gianni's back pocket. When Gianni was out of sight, Vito opened his tin and dropped the coins in alongside the cigarettes. Then he looked down into the valley and saw a train pulling into the station. Black smoke was billowing from its stack, filling the sky.

The musicians, identical in their white, short-sleeved shirts and black trousers, tumbled out of the carriages carrying their instruments. They stretched and looked around. A couple of them unloaded two, shiny brass kettle-drums and set them down on the platform.

Alessandro, Vito's cousin, led his mule towards the kettle-drums. Its hooves clicked over the smooth, unfamiliar surface. Alessandro tied its rein to one of the uprights that supported the station awning. Then he acknowledged the two musicians, who were emerging from the carriage again, each carrying a brass cymbal and its stand. He shook hands with them, then lifted the kettle-drums onto the mule's saddle and fastened them with some leather straps. After eyeing the load carefully, he arranged the cymbals and stands between the drums and secured them too. When he was done, the mule shifted itself and eeaawed complainingly, accustoming itself to the weight, then pissed copiously over the platform.

'He always waits until he's loaded before he pisses' Alessandro said, grinning.

Drawn by the sound of workmen erecting a bandstand, Vito made his way to the Piazza. A stage was being built, with poles around the edge where lamps would be hung. Mariella was leading Pina, her younger sister, by the hand. Vito would've gone over, if he hadn't been so sweaty and smelling of fireworks. He retreated into a side-street instead. Mariella and Pina walked by, unaware of him. Mariella was wearing perfume which unsettled Vito. When they were out of sight, he ran home.

Vito's mother was sitting in the door-way, fast asleep in a chair. Her dress was unbuttoned exposing one of her breasts. His baby brother was asleep in the crook of her arm. Vito heard a couple of men approaching, talking loudly and stood in front of her so they wouldn't see. When they'd passed, he touched her shoulder gently.

'Vito,' she said, blinking.

The baby began to cry. His mother pulled open the other side of her dress, exposing both her breasts and switched him to the other side.

'Do you have to do that out on the street?' Vito asked.

She didn't reply. When the baby had drunk enough and was falling asleep, she buttoned her dress, then took him inside and settled him into his cradle.

Vito took off his shirt and dropped it on the floor. Then he cranked the pump and started washing himself.

'You'll have to wear your shirt a little longer,' his mother said. 'I haven't washed your other one yet.'

'That's all right, I'll wear my good shirt.' He lathered the soap in his hands and worked it over his chest.

'Your good shirt is for Sundays,' she said, looking away.

'But the band is on its way from the station.'

She picked up his shirt and checked the buttons, then smelled it. 'Are you meeting someone.'

'No!'

'Shush…' She touched her lips. 'You'll wake your brother.'

'But… I can't go like this,' he said, pointing at his patched trousers.

'You want to wear your good trousers too?'

'Yes…'

'Are you sure you're not meeting someone?'

'Yes… I'm not meeting anyone.' He looked away, unlaced his boots and took them off.

'All right… You can wear your good clothes.' She smiled, then picked up his boots and left.

Vito finished washing and changed. Then he wetted his hair and combed it in front of a mirror. When he came out, he saw his polished boots by the door and put them on. His mother was outside sitting in her chair, talking to her sister, Alessandro's mother.

'Where's Alessandro today?' Vito asked.

'He got up early and went with the mule to help the musicians with their drums,' she replied.

'Oh! In that case, I'll go to the Piazza in case he needs a hand,' Vito said. He kissed his aunt, then went on his way.

A crowd had gathered in the Piazza, admiring the completed bandstand. Mariella was there too, still leading Pina by the hand. She smiled at Vito.

He smiled back and went over.

'Are you coming to see the band tonight?' he asked. Then he smelled her perfume again and began stumbling over his words.

Pina noticed and stuck out her tongue.

Mariella raised her hand, as if she were going to slap her.

Pina flinched, then stared sulkily at the ground.

'It depends on my father,' Mariella said.

Alessandro entered the Piazza with his mule strutting petulantly behind him. The cymbals and kettle-drums veered from side to side, catching the sun. There was a commotion and laughter in the crowd, then someone threw a lighted firework in the mule's direction. The mule let out a high pitched eeaaw, before rearing up on its hind legs. Alessandro pulled down on the reins.

'Take it easy,' Alessandro repeated, until the banging stopped. 'Vito… Can you hold him for me?' he called.

The mule flicked its hooves.

Alessandro punched its nose. It shook its head, then whined fitfully.

Vito left Mariella and Pina, then skirted around the mule's rear end, and wound the reins around his hand, happy that they were watching.

Alessandro unfastened the cymbals and handed them to the musicians, then he unfastened one of the kettle-drums and lowered it to the ground. His shirt was torn and soaked with sweat.

Mariella stared at him, unable to help herself.

The mule stamped on the cobbles, adjusting itself to accommodate the imbalance. Then it planted its hooves firmly on the ground and began flexing its belly, until its penis slipped out from its sheathing, huge and pink, with knots of dark blue veins running down its sides.

Mariella's face turned white.

The mule eeaawed forlornly, then pissed on the cobbles.

'Ugh! Look,' Pina said, pointing. 'It's making a mess.'

Alessandro looked round and saw Mariella staring at the monster, swinging pendulously beneath his mule's belly and grinned. She turned towards him, long enough for a look to pass between them, then grabbed Pina's hand and strode off.

'Will I see you tonight?' Vito called out.

Mariella broke into a run, dragging Pina along behind her without replying.

Alessandro unloaded the second kettle-drum and set it down next to its partner.

'Do you have a cigarette?' Alessandro asked.

'Sure.' Vito opened his tin and offered his cigarettes.

Alessandro looked at them.

'Take one of the un-smoked ones,' Vito said.

Alessandro did so and Vito took the part-smoked one. Then Alessandro produced a match from his pocket, struck it on the sole of his boot and cupped his hands around the yellow flame.

Vito stepped forward and drew on his cigarette.

'Are you seeing Mariella tonight?' Alessandro asked, then he lit his own cigarette and blew out the smoke.

'I'm not sure. It depends on her father,' Vito replied. He shrugged and his face flushed.

***

Vito carried their cases up to the first floor.

The owner of the pension threw open the door and gestured for them to enter. The room was white-washed and clean-smelling, with an iron bedstead beneath a window. There was a wardrobe against one wall and a dressing table against the other. Both were white, with brown varnish showing through where the paint had flaked.

'My wife will bring up a jug of hot water at seven,' the pension owner said.

He pointed to an iron wash-stand, with a white china bowl. There were white towels draped either side and a bar of strong-smelling, white soap in a scallop holder.

Pearl gave Vito a look.

'Can we have the hot water at eight?' Vito asked.

'Eight!' the pension owner repeated.

'Yes… And where is the bathroom?'

'At the end of the hall-way.'

The pension owner looked Pearl up and down, then left.

Pearl sat on the bed, taking in the room, then she rolled back the starched, fresh-smelling covers. 'Well, at least everything is clean,' she said.

Vito nodded, visibly relieved.

Pearl opened the window and looked out. 'There are donkeys and mules tied to the walls,' she said, wrinkling her nose. 'They're doing their business all over the street!'

'I told you it would still be pretty backward,' he said.

'That's twice you've said that today...' She looked out of the window again and pointed inquisitively. 'What are those men doing over there?'

He looked across the rooftops to where the village fell away and saw a couple of men, bent over, working. 'Looks like they're setting up the fireworks for tonight.'

'Fireworks!' Pearl's face lit up.

'Yes. And there'll be a band.'

***

The lamps had been lit and burned above the stage. A moth flapped in out of the darkness, singed its wings and fell smouldering to the ground. Vito felt the crowd pressing in on him, then someone touched his back. He smelled Mariella's perfume and turned around. Pina was standing between them, grinning.

'I can't see,' Pina shouted. Her hair was wound into two plaits, which stuck out either side of her head.

Vito smiled at her, then at Mariella. They both smiled back.

Pina held up her arms, 'Pick me up...please.' she whined, then smiled again.

Mariella nodded, which he took as approval and lifted Pina up onto his shoulders.

The conductor tapped the lectern with his baton. The musicians looked up, then started to play.

Pina started swaying around in time with the music.

Mariella looked up at her, then moved closer to Vito and held his arm...

The final piece of music, when it eventually came, after many encores, was followed by the screech of fireworks and loud bangs. The crowd gasped, then began funnelling themselves through the narrow streets.

'Let's go and see the fireworks,' Pina shouted. She was pulling Vito's hair and steering him with her knees.

The street was unlit. Only the faces close by them were visible. Pina's sweaty legs were sticking to Vito's neck. He pushed his hands under her armpits and raised her up.

'No! I want to stay here,' she protested.

He lowered her back down onto his shoulders.

Lamps had been placed at intervals along the top of the village wall. The fortunate, early arrivals sat between them with their legs dangling over. Vito looked along the wall and saw Alessandro a long way off, sitting with a couple of friends, talking and laughing. One of the friends passed round a packet of cigarettes, then he struck a match and they all lit up. When they'd finished smoking Alessandro shook hands with them and left.

A silver fireball rose into the sky, followed by an explosion, then burst into silver flares. Vito looked down to where he'd helped Gianni set up the fireworks and saw his unmistakeable silhouette, moving around among them.

'Look! Look!' Pina shouted, waving her arms.

The sky filled with a mass of coloured star-bursts. Feeling that he was neglecting Mariella, he turned toward her despite Pina's protests. Unable to see her, or smell her perfume, he looked into the crowd, as far as the darkness allowed.

Pina pulled his hair and dug her heels into his chest. 'Turn around. Turn around. I can't see,' she shouted.

Vito endured until the silence eventually came, along with a moan from the crowd.

Pina scrambled down from his shoulders. He pulled at his shirt. The night air cooled his skin.

'Where's Mariella?' Pina asked, looking into the darkness… 'Where's Mariella?'

Vito looked around at the dispersing crowd, then tried to take her hand.

She snatched it way.

'She'll be in the Piazza… by the bandstand,' he said, not knowing what else to say. 'Come on…We'll meet her there.'

He held out his hand again.

'She'd better be there,' she said, then took his hand reluctantly.

The lamps were still burning above the bandstand, lighting the abandoned stage.

'You said she'd be here,' Pina said. Her face began to quiver.

He looked around the darkened Piazza.

Eventually there was a sound, like a cat meowing.

'Vito! Where have you been?' Mariella shrieked, running out of the darkness. Her face was red and her dress was dishevelled. She threw her arms around Pina and started sobbing. 'The crowd pushed us apart…' she said, looking at Vito. 'I shouted, but you didn't hear me! Then I lost sight of you. I've been searching all night!'

Pina glared at him, then her face crumpled and she started sobbing too.

Eventually, Mariella calmed down. She took a handkerchief from her pocket and wiped Pina's tears. 'We can't go home like this,' she said, laughing nervously. 'It must have been the noise of the fireworks. That's why you didn't hear me calling, Vito.' She wiped her eyes, then blew her nose, then she shook her head and squeezed his arm.

He breathed in her perfume which added to his confusion.

'I was frightened. I didn't mean to shout at you earlier,' she said, shaking her head. Her face and neck were flushed. She looked up into his eyes. 'Will you walk home with us?'

Vito nodded, not knowing what else to do. He went with them as far as their street.

Mariella tightened her grip on his arm. 'Leave us here,' she said, then kissed his cheek and let him go.

Vito stood in the shadows while she knocked on the door. The door opened, followed by her father's shouting, then a brief silence, until all Vito could hear was her inevitable crying.

Alessandro was sitting on the stage, beneath the now extinguished lamps. He was drinking from a bottle and grinned broadly as Vito approached him. He passed Vito the bottle, then produced a packet of cigarettes from his pocket and offered him one.

Vito fumbled with the packet and pulled one out.

Alessandro struck a match and cupped the yellow flame in his hands, letting it illuminate Vito's face.

Vito drew on the cigarette. Then, as the sulphur smell dissipated, he thought he smelled Mariella's perfume again! He passed the bottle back to Alessandro.

Alessandro took it and drank, until the bottle was empty, then he stood the bottle between them and lay down on the stage, staring up at the sky.

Vito waited until he started snoring, then leaned over, close enough to smell him better and smelled Mariella's unmistakable perfume again! A taste like rusty iron filled his mouth, then spread into his chest. Barely able to breathe, he picked up the empty bottle as if he had no choice and gripped it by the neck, as though it were a club.

***

'What's that statue they're carrying over there?' Pearl asked.

'St Francis,' Vito replied.

'You mean St Francis of Assisi!?'

'Yes… That's right.'

One of her stilettos slipped between the cobbles. 'Can we join in the procession,' she asked, grabbing his arm.

Vito propped her up.

The people in the procession stared at her.

She stopped, self-consciously, long enough to take a blue head-scarf from her handbag and put it on.

The statue of St Francis swayed around above the priests' shoulders. A smaller statue of the Virgin Mary, wearing a blue shawl, almost identical in colour to Pearl's head-scarf, was placed at St Francis's feet.

Pearl's face broke into a brief, self-satisfied smile until her stiletto slipped between the cobbles again, twisting her ankle.

'Do we have to follow right to the end?' Vito asked.

'Where does it end?' she replied.

'Over there.' He pointed to a church close-by.

'Oh! I think I should be able to make it that far.'

The procession did an about-turn.

'What's happening?' Pearl asked.

'The procession goes all over the village, until every street has been blessed,' Vito replied.

'Oh! Well in that case it may be better to wait here and pick it up at the end,' she said.

***

Vito scrambled down to where he'd helped set up the fireworks. Their burnt-out smell pricked his nostrils. He kicked one. Some orange sparks rose up out of its black, burnt-out husk. He looked disbelievingly at the broken bottle, before throwing it as far away as he could, then scrambled back up to the village.

A lamp was burning over the door of the pension where Gianni was staying. Vito went towards it. The door was locked and the window shutters closed. He went around the back. Gianni was snoring on a make-shift bed in an open stable. An oil-lamp was burning from a rafter above his head and an empty wine bottle lay on the floor beside him. A donkey scuffled in its stall, followed by a sound like loose change jingling as its bridle-chain adjusted to its movements. Vito slowed his breathing in time with Gianni's snoring. Gianni turned over onto his side, exposing his rolled-up trousers sticking out from under his pillow. Vito waited until he settled and resumed his snoring. Then he moved closer, gently removed the trousers and felt through the pockets until he found the wallet.

The street was empty. He heard footsteps and looked over his shoulder. The footsteps stopped. He carried on. The footsteps continued. He stopped again and kicked the cobbles. An echo rang out, then died away. His breath was short and his heart was pounding. Certain that no one was following, he considered going home to count the money, then changed his mind and took the wallet out of his pocket. It smelled of leather and reminded him of Gianni. Unable to bear the smell, he removed the money, put it in his pocket and dropped the wallet into the gutter.

**

'I think that old guy is staring at us,' Pearl said.

'Where?' Vito looked around.

'Stop. Or he'll think we're staring at him… The old guy with the scars over his face.'

The old guy was sitting in his doorway. He eyed them inquisitively, then he forced himself up out of his chair and walked over, leaning heavily on a stick. He looked Vito up and down, while studying Pearl surreptitiously.

Pearl smoothed her dress.

The procession reappeared, passing close by them. The priests were chanting in Latin. The three of them looked on silently, until the procession did an about-turn and moved on, into yet another street.

'Americano?' the old guy asked, breaking the silence that had formed between them.

'Just her,' Vito replied. 'I was born here.'

The old guy looked closely at Vito's face, then shook his head. 'Cataracts,' he said, pointing at his eyes. 'I don't recognise anyone any more. How long have you been away?'

'Many years,' Vito answered.

'Hmm… have you come back to retire?' the old guy asked, squinting badly.

'No,' Vito replied.

An obese old woman, dressed in black, appeared in the doorway where the old guy had been sitting. She folded her broad forearms over her breasts. 'I thought I told you to go fetch some oil,' she shouted.

'For Christ's sake,' the old guy shouted back. 'Mariella, can't you see I'm talking to someone.' Then he muttered something neither Vito nor Pearl could understand and wandered off.

'Did you know those people!?' Pearl asked.

Vito watched as Mariella turned around and went back into the house. 'Not that I recollect…'

'Is something wrong?' Pearl asked.

'No.'

'Are you sure you didn't know them? It's like they're from another world.'

'I told you it would still be pretty backward,' Vito replied.

'You keep saying that…'

'Well, it was *your* idea to come here,' Vito said.

A tear rolled down Pearl's face… 'I just wanted to see where you were born,' she said.

They were both quiet.

'Are you sure you don't have any family here?' Pearl asked.

'Maybe an odd cousin but no one very close.'

They were quiet again.

'My ankles are hurting,' she said, needing to break the silence. 'Can we leave the procession and go back to the pension?

'Are you sure you don't want to wait until it ends!?'

'No… it's all right,' she replied, leaning heavily on him. 'I'm feeling blessed enough as it is.'

***

Vito stopped at each hair-pin bend and looked up at the village. Alessandro hadn't seen him break the bottle into his face and Gianni hadn't seen him either. He considered returning and denying all knowledge. He held the money in his hand, wondering where to hide it. He considered throwing it away. Then eventually, after considering what it would be like to lie for the rest of his life, he put it back into his pocket.

***

'Do you think I look Ok in these?' Pearl asked, pointing down at the flat canvass shoes she'd just bought.

'Yes… but it'd be better if you didn't wear the pants.'

She looked in the mirror and smoothed her hands over her hips. 'You mean they don't go?'

'It's not that,' he paused, looking for the right words. 'It's more that the women around here don't usually wear pants.'

'You mean: "It's still pretty backward around here,"' she said, mimicking him.

He didn't reply.

She searched through her dresses, sighing, then took a beige two-piece outfit off the hanger and held it in front of her. She put it on, looked in the mirror and sighed again. Then she sat down and stared at her reflection. A moment later she leaned hard against the glass, examining her hair.

'It must be the sun!'

'What do you mean?' he asked.

'Look… the roots are OK, but the white is coming through the ends!'

***

Apart from the ticket-seller sitting outside the ticket office smoking a cigarette, the station was deserted. Vito nodded vaguely in his direction, then went into the toilet.

The floor was wet and smelled of urine. He closed the door, dropped his pants and sat down. The diarrhoea poured out of him. He sat for a while massaging his abdomen until the numbness subsided. Then he washed his hands. He went back into the cubicle, closed the door again, took the money out of his pocket and tried to count it. Unable to concentrate, he peeled off one of the notes instead and put it in his tin, laying it over the coins Gianni had given him, then he pushed the remainder deeply into his pocket and returned to the platform.

'Can I buy cigarettes here?' he asked the ticket seller, with as much self-confidence as he could muster. He slapped his pockets as though searching for something.

The ticket-seller looked him up and down, raising his eyebrows. 'No, but have one of these.' He produced a packet of cigarettes from his shirt pocket.

Vito took one.

The ticket-seller produced a lighter from the same pocket and flicked it open. 'Where are you going?' he asked, holding the blue flame up towards Vito.

'Rome.' It was the first place Vito could think of.

'What for?'

'To work,'

'Do you have a job there?'

'Not yet...' Vito drew on his cigarette... 'I'm going to look for one.'

'There's no work in Rome,' the ticket-seller said. 'Or anywhere else.'

The ticket-seller stood up and went into the ticket office.

'A single to Rome,' Vito said.

The ticket-seller smiled. 'Listen,' he said. 'If you get a return ticket it'll save you money and you'll be able to come back whenever you want.'

'A single ticket will be fine,' Vito replied, taking the note from his tin and pushing it under the glass screen.

The ticket-seller took it, shaking his head, then gave him the ticket, along with a couple of smaller notes and some coins in change.

Vito walked off, putting the notes and ticket into his tin, then he replaced the lid and shook it. The coins rattled.

'When will the train come?' he called to the ticket-seller, who was back sitting in his chair, smoking.

'Soon,' the ticket-seller replied. 'Unless it's late.'

***

Walking a little more comfortably, Pearl crossed the Piazza, hanging on to Vito's arm. It was early evening and she'd put on the blue head-scarf she'd worn for the procession. They walked past the bandstand enjoying the evening air. Then they sat down at one of the two tables outside the only trattoria in the village,

The owner, a thin, handsome-looking old man, around Vito's age, came out with a bottle of water in one hand and a bottle of red wine in the other.

'Buona sera,' he said and nodded politely.

He put the bottles on the table, then set the four glasses upright and poured the wine, then he poured the water. The wine was red and strong-smelling. He nodded again and left.

'Where's the menu?' Pearl asked.

'I don't think there is one,' Vito replied.

Pearl pulled a face, then she picked up the glass of wine and held it under her nose. She made another face that Vito couldn't read, then took a small sip of the wine, swilled it around her mouth and swallowed. A puzzled look came over her face. She took another sip and smiled.

Vito smiled too and sighed with relief.

The waiter returned with two bowls of pasta, generously covered in thick tomato sauce. He set Pearl's bowl down, then Vito's, and returned inside.

Pearl followed him with her eyes, noticing his clean, well-pressed but shabby clothes.

He returned with a cheese grater and a block of Parmesan, smiled at them both, then began grating Parmesan over Pearl's pasta.

A lock of hair had worked its way out from under her scarf. She worked it back under, then looked up at the waiter and smiled.

He took that as his cue to stop grating and turned towards Vito.

She studied the waiter's hands surreptitiously as he worked the Parmesan over the grater. They were gnarled and heavily veined, like a labourer's. She stared at his face, unable to help herself, as the flakes settled like snow over Vito's pasta.

Vito nodded.

The waiter tapped the Parmesan against the grater and looked up.

Pearl blushed, then looked down at her bowl and began eating.

The light was starting to fade when the waiter returned to clear their plates. He went off, then returned with a bowl of fresh, neatly-cut fennel for them to share. Pearl was picking at the fennel and checking her watch, wondering if the meal was over, when he reappeared with two medium steaks. He was followed by an old woman dressed in black, bearing a bowl of fries.

The old woman reminded Pearl of the woman on the donkey they'd passed earlier.

She put the bowl of fries on the table, then nodded meekly.

Pearl nodded back, wondering if it was all right to smile.

The old woman twisted her hands into her white apron and left.

'Her apron was spotless!' Pearl whispered. 'Do you think they're married?'

'Either that or they're brother and sister,' Vito replied.

'Brother and sister!?'

'Yes. The village is full of old spinsters.'

'How come?'

'Emigration.'

The waiter returned with a lamp, lit it and left it in the centre of their table. A moth flapped in out of the twilight, singed its wings, then smouldered helplessly on the table cloth. Pearl and Vito stared at each other over the empty wine bottle.

'Shall we order another?' Pearl asked. Her speech was slurred and more of her hair had fallen out from under her scarf.

'If you want to,' Vito replied.

'Do you want to?'

'Only if you do.'

The waiter returned and cleared the plates.

Vito ordered another bottle of wine.

'We can always take it back to the pension,' Pearl said. 'Oh! Look over there.'

The electric lamps strung over the bandstand had come on and the musicians were tuning their instruments.

The waiter returned with the wine, poured it and left. Pearl drank most of her glass in one long swallow, then leaned back into her chair.

'We can watch the performance from here,' she said, smiling in anticipation. 'The view is perfect.'

Vito looked around the Piazza. People were starting to mill around. Some mosquitoes began hovering around Pearl's head. She batted them away with the edge of her hand, catching her scarf. More of her hair fell out from under it.

'Ask them where the rest-room is will you? These bugs are eating me alive,' she shouted, adjusting her scarf with both hands.

The old woman heard the commotion and appeared in the doorway.

Vito called her over.

The old woman took in the situation at a glance and helped Pearl out of her chair. She staggered with her to the door and took her inside. The waiter was sitting in a chair, smoking. A look passed between him and the old woman. Pearl made the effort to stand upright and unsupported. The old woman led her by the hand through her living-room, past the shabby furniture. They stopped in front of a mahogany chiffonier, covered with generations of cheaply-framed, family photographs. The old woman waited until Pearl was ready, then urged her along and opened a door.

The coldness of the marble floor worked its way through Pearl's canvass shoes. The old woman helped her to a stone sink, then removed a metal bowl with her underwear soaking in it. She placed the bowl on the floor, next to a chair with a pile of clean, neatly folded white towels on it. Pearl grasped the sink with both hands and stared at her refection in the oval mirror hanging above it.

'I'm all right now,' Pearl said impatiently, vaguely gesturing something with her hands.

The old woman nodded in her usual way and left.

Pearl's scarf was rucked up at one side and her hair stuck out in a tangle from under it. She tried unsuccessfully to tuck it back under, then pulled off the scarf and unfastened the knot. She fumbled in her hand-bag, found her hair-brush and brushed furiously until her hair was flat against her head and touching her shoulders. She stared at the pump, wondering how it worked, then cranked it harder than she needed to. More water gushed out than she was expecting. After it drained away, she dampened her handkerchief and removed her make-up. Then, cupping her hands under the flow, she washed her face and neck until she was shivering. She dried herself with one of the towels. She looked at her reflection, shaking her head disapprovingly, then reapplied her make-up, fixed her hair and tied the scarf back over it.

The old woman was sitting in a high-backed wooden chair, with her hands in her lap, crocheting something. The waiter was standing by the stove. There was a hissing sound and a smell of coffee. The waiter turned off the stove and looked Pearl up and down. Pearl touched her scarf and forced a smile. The old woman stopped crocheting and stared at the wool. Pearl mustered herself and walked unaided through the kitchen, back to the table.

A thick, heavily scented candle had been lit and placed on the table.

'They should've lit that to begin with,' Pearl said, sitting upright on the edge of her chair. 'That way I needn't have made a fool of myself.' She took a compact out of her hand-bag and checked her scarf again in the mirror.

The old woman appeared with a tray. She placed a cup of coffee down in front of each of them and a bowl of round, sweet biscuits. Pearl drank some water, then sipped her coffee. She relaxed back into her chair and ate one of the biscuits. The sugar revived her. She checked her scarf and started smiling again.

'See. I was right about the view!' she said.

The Piazza was teeming with people. She pointed over their heads to the musicians on the raised-up stage. Their shiny instruments were swaying in time with the music.

The old woman and the waiter sat down at the other table.

'They look done for the night,' Pearl whispered, then poured herself some more wine.

Eventually, after many encores the concert ended.

'Where's everyone going?' Pearl asked.

'To see the fireworks,' Vito replied.

'Can we go too?'

'We'll be able to see them just as well from here,' Vito said.

'Oh no! Not after coming all this way.' Pearl stood up, swayed around a little, then gripped the edge of the table.

The waiter glanced at her.

Vito stood up and held her arm.

She leaned into him.

Vito reached into his pocket with his free hand, pulled out some money and laid it on the table, then stood the empty wine-bottle on top.

'I don't know what their problem was,' Pearl said.

'What do you mean?' They were in a side-street with the crowd pressing in on them, moving along with the flow.

'Didn't you notice the way they were looking at us? Where are we going anyway? I can hardly see a thing. They should put some street-lights up around here!'

'Over there, to the village wall.'

She leaned against Vito, standing on tip-toes. She saw the wall at the end of the street, lit up by coloured light bulbs, strung from make-shift poles. The fortunate early arrivals were sitting on the wall with their legs dangling over.

'I just saw them again,' she said.

'Who?'

'That scar-faced man and his wife. Look, they're still arguing!'

Vito looked over.

Mariella was red-faced and shouting.

Alessandro held out his open palms.

Mariella shouted some more.

Alessandro turned his back in desperation.

The sky filled with fireworks, exploding noisily in all directions.

Mariella clenched her fists desperately and pounded his back.

'Aren't you glad you're not married to someone like that!' Pearl shouted.

Vito nodded and smiled agreeably.

Pearl huffed as though lost for words, then pressed her hands down on her scarf and ran her fingers around the edge, checking her hair.

Printed in Great Britain
by Amazon

36199050R00071